Two Worlds

FOR GAVIN

Two Worlds

Written by

Laura T. Lee

Laura T Lee

Infomages Publishing

2018

Two Worlds

Written by young author Laura T. Lee at age 10.

Infomages Publishing, PO Box 182, Northborough, MA 01532 USA

Or, email to:

samlee@infomages.com

Library of Congress Cataloging-in-Publication Data (will be available upon LOC approval)

ISBN-13: 978-1534927513
ISBN-10: 1534927514

Published by:
Infomages Publishing, PO Box 182, Northborough, MA 01532 USA

Printed in the United States of America

First edition first printing, July 2016

For more information, please visit http://infomages.com/booksrfun/.

Dedication

This book is dedicated to my family and my grandparents, who supported me in the production of this book.

Summary of the story

Fifteen-year-old Lily Claire isn't a violent person. When she is taken from Earth to another planet known as the elfin world, she starts a war she cannot stop. She will plunge into dangerous challenges, putting her life on the line along with many others. One misstep, and things go extremely wrong. The enemies change constantly, from deadly dwarves to sorceress sisters. If only Lily could ask someone for tips on defeating the enemies. Oh, wait! No one has ever defeated these enemies before. As an innocent teenager, Lily has no place in wars. Unfortunately, she has no choice but to join in. This story is about an ongoing fight against evil and taking risks to save lives.

Inventory of characters

Lily Claire

Human teenager who is taken to the elfin world

Jake Iander

War general, works in the elfin central tower

Tara Aiwa

Battle officer/soldier, also works in the elfin central tower

Stacy Dana

Manager of the elfin control center

Oneida Iander

Jake's younger sister, a war medic

Parker Iander

Jake's older brother, a battle officer/soldier

Theresa Foveae

Elf sorceress, imprisoned in a locked palace for fifty years

Sophie Foveae

Elf sorceress, locked her sister Theresa in a prison for fifty years, leads invasion on Earth against Lily and her friends

Table of Contents

PART 2: THERESA, THE QUEEN

PART 1:

The ELFIN WORLD

Chapter 1

A school catastrophe

Ding! The lunch bell rang and fifteen-year-old Lily Claire headed back to her classroom. She grabbed her iPad from her backpack before walking to her desk. As Lily sat down in her seat their teacher, Ms. Anne, tapped her ruler on the whiteboard. "Okay, class!" she said. "Log on to your iPad and we'll begin our lesson." Lily turned on her tablet and typed in her password: Schoolgirl72. The password bar turned red. Access denied was placed over it.

Access denied? She'd been using that password for one and a half years! Her iPad never did that. More words formed next to the password bar. iPad blocked. What was going on? "Uh ... Ms. Anne?" Lily called. Her teacher appeared not to have heard. In fact, none of Lily's class seemed to be moving. Hands hovered over tablets. Someone who decided to jump into their seat was frozen in mid-air, his feet half a foot from the ground. Only Lily could move properly.

But wait! More words had appeared on her iPad. Override password initiated, it read. Lily blinked. "Huh?" The tablet screen turned neon gray and the light wrapped Lily in a cocoon of energy. "What's going on?" she muttered as the gray light around her suddenly turned blindingly bright. Lily was knocked unconscious.

Two seconds after Lily closed her eyes, a young woman entered the room. A taller cloaked man around the same age followed closely behind. Both had pointed ears. "Are you sure she is the right one?" the man asked. The lady turned to face him. "Jake, she must be the right one, otherwise, we wouldn't have spent two years searching, would we?" The woman briskly snapped her fingers and Lily vanished in a flash of more intense neon gray light. Around the man and woman, teenagers began to move in slow motion, gradually returning to normal. "Tara, we should go," Jake said. "The time freeze is wearing off." Tara and Jake quickly exited the classroom.

***

Lily woke up on a slab of cold hard stone and groaned. She opened her eyes and ... wait a second. This was definitely not her school.

Blinding white walls surrounded her. Lily was alone.

"Uh...hello?" she called.

"Hello!" a high-pitched voice answered.

A hidden door opened to reveal a small child, no more than five years old. She had an adorable face, with short auburn hair curling around the sides of her head. "Follow me!" she said. Lily got up and followed the girl out of the room.

The little girl led Lily down a long hallway to a stone door. "In here," she said. The child rippled into a group of rapidly vanishing pixels. A hologram?

Lily blinked in confusion. "Hello?" her voice echoed down the empty corridor. Perplexed, she pushed open the stone door. She entered a cavernous room with colossal windows. The one piece of furniture inside was a small table with a variety of weapons - swords, blasters, and buttons - covering it. Lily reached out to touch a pink button. "A voice behind her said, "Careful."

Lily turned and spotted the tall cloaked figure of a man. He made no attempt to move. "I wouldn't touch those buttons if I were you. They're smart bombs activated by touch. You would go BOOM!" he explained. Lily winced. "Who are you?" she asked. "I am Jake," he said. "You must be Lily."

Lily snapped back to her senses. "Where am I?" she demanded. "Are ... are you aliens?"

(Yeah, whatever, that was a stupid question.)

Jake sniffed indignantly. "I am not an *alien*," he said. "We are part of a planet similar to Earth, and we don't have any differences to humans except for our pointed ears, so if you wouldn't terribly mind, call us elves." He sounded like a college professor, just without the English accent.

(Technically, elves are aliens, but that's not the point of the story!)

Lily tried to think of something polite to say. She couldn't.

Jake smiled. "Our kind is ... the most intelligent version of humans. But if you please, I do not wish to be called an alien ever again." He said the word alien as though it were a slimy rat, wrinkling his nose in disgust. The expression froze on Jake's face.

For a while, Lily stared at Jake. The elf (what else could she call him?) finally seemed to notice that Lily was looking at him like he was a madman. Embarrassed, he cleared his throat - *cough!* - and shifted his facial features to a friendly smile. "Uh ... Let's start with a tour!" he said.

Turns out an elf tour meant going to the P.O.O.P.

The first time Jake had mentioned the acronym Lily had considered him an "exceedingly rude person", as her mother would say. Then Jake said: "P.O.O.P means the Post Office for Oversized Packages, not including dwarves (long story). Did you know that our people made a peace treaty with the dwarves thousands of years ago? Anyway, this service includes transportation of vehicles, ships, airplanes and of course, the occasional prisoner (no food or drinks are allowed). Also, packages are ... WATCH OUT!" He said that last part because Lily nearly stepped on a puddle of 'intergalactic slime' as Jake proclaimed. "Hazardous material," Jake explained. *Ugh*, Lily thought with a shudder.

The two finally arrived at a P.O.O.P station. A deserted booth with a button on top stood in front of a cube-shaped elevator. "Where is everyone?" Lily asked. "They were evacuated to the main city because they thought you were a Fighter," Jake said. "Not that you are," he added. "What's a Fighter?" Lily asked. "Somebody who brings doom to all elfin people by fighting and other kinds of violence," Jake said, as though it were obvious. "Are you actually an alien ... er, elf?" Lily asked. Jake gave her an irritated look like *well, duh*! He reached out and tapped the button.

A hidden door slid open on the elevator box. Jake promptly shoved a confused Lily into the container before jumping in himself. The door slammed shut. Nothing happened. After five minutes of total silence, Lily was just about to ask Jake if the elevator had broken down when the door in front of them opened. The two climbed out to a nearly pitch-black area. "Uh ... where are we, exactly?" Lily asked. Her voice echoed eerily off what seemed to be walls. Next to Lily, Jake shifted uncomfortably. "Darn it. Must be nighttime," he muttered. Suddenly, someone grabbed Lily and stabbed a needle into her arm. Nearby, she heard Jake fall to the ground with a yell of surprise, out for the count. I hate getting knocked out, Lily thought as she slumped to the floor.

***

"Hello?" Lily's eyes groggily opened to find a lady alien (oh, dang it, elf) looking at her. She had auburn hair - like that little girl who first met her - that tumbled down her shoulders. Lily was lying down on another hard slab, only with comfy cushions.

Lily tried to say something. "Unnngh." Whoops. Apparently, her voice wasn't working. The woman frowned. "Hmm," she said. "The sleeping potion hasn't worn off yet. But just so you know, when your voice comes back, you may call me Tara." Lily tried to talk again. "Um ... I can talk now." Tara smiled. "Excellent!" she said. "Welcome to the Special Infirmary. Do you have any questions?" In fact, Lily had a million things to ask Tara, like why am I not totally freaking out right now? But one question stood out from the rest. "I am starving. Do you have any food in this place?"

Chapter 2

The humans who never were

As soon as Lily had finished eating her meal (she didn't even know what time it was) two burly armored guards took her to a small meeting room. Jake was waiting for her. He smiled as Lily appeared at the door. "My apologies," he said. "The guards are quite a bit sensitive to unknown newcomers, even if one of their own is guiding them." Jake shot a very irritated look at the elves holding Lily. It was then that Lily spotted a tiny syringe in a tiny holster on each guard. Jake waved his hand to dismiss the guards.

"Now," he said. "I suppose you're wondering why I summoned you to this room." *You're a genius!* Lily thought. "Do you recognize these two men?" Jake asked. He pointed to two paintings of men in wigs on a nearby table.

Lily puzzled, studied the pictures. "Uh ... yes, I do," she said. "George Washington and John Adams?" "Yes," Jake said. "Am I correct that they are American heroes?" Lily nodded. "I see," Jake said, "How about now?" He pointed to two more pictures of the same men. Lily didn't see any difference until she saw they had pointed ears.

"Eeep!" Lily covered her mouth as the sound escaped her lips. "They're aliens!" Jake sighed in exasperation. "Yes, these famous men were elves," he said. "They wore wigs to cover their ears, if you didn't already know. Tons of humans used to think that they were just old, but elves and pixies can live over 100 years old. I, for example, am 157 years old." Jake certainly didn't look like a 157-year-old person - he looked as though he were twenty-five.

Soon, Jake began to show Lily more pictures of famous 'humans'. These profiles included Benjamin Franklin (Oh, really?) Abraham Lincoln (That's weird) Marilyn Monroe (What the-) and the host of the show 'Yo Gabba Gabba!' (BLEAUGH!!)

Ten minutes later, a horrified Lily managed to exit the room. As she walked through the hall back to her living quarters, Lily's feet began to trip over one another. Her eyelids drooped with fatigue. Lily barely managed to stumble to her bed before falling over. She was asleep before her head hit the pillow, which was fine, as long as she didn't snore.

Boom. Lily sat up in bed. What was that sound? Boom. Boom. CRASH! The deafening sound of breaking and splintering wood traveled down the hall. Lily flinched. Footsteps clomped down the hall. The noise stopped at the door nest to Lily's. A loud crack sound could be heard as the door slammed open. A voice scowled loudly. "Nobody here," he said. The footsteps continued to Lily's door. Crack! The door swung open.

Lily found herself looking at a small group of people, clad in black. They had black ski masks over their heads, and their eyes peeked out at her. They snarled silently and approached. Nobody noticed a shadow in the hallway.

The next moment, Tara had appeared in the middle of the group, punching and kicking until every little person was down. She rushed to Lily's side. "Are you all right?" Tara asked. Lily nodded.

Chapter 2: The humans who never were

Due to safety concerns, Lily was transferred to the Special Infirmary, where she could sleep for the rest of the night. It seemed only a few seconds since she had closed her eyes before she was woken up to the sound of yelling and clattering footsteps. Lily looked out the doorway just in time to see several armed elves rush by. A few seconds later, an unfamiliar girl close to Lily's age (but for all she knew, the teen could've been 100) came in and started to clear the area of people.

"What's going on?" Lily asked as the girl passed by. "The east wall has been breached and the security guards aren't responding so the infirmary must be evacuated," the girl said, looking at her. "That includes you, miss." *Nope*, Lily thought. When the girl wasn't looking she swung her legs out of bed and raced out the open door.

The hallway was strangely empty as Lily ran past random doors. She sprinted up a flight of stairs, turned a corner and dashed straight into Tara.

Tara yelped in surprise. "What are you doing here?" she asked. "I just wanted-" Lily started to talk but her voice drained away as Tara's eyes locked on something behind her. Lily spun around on her heel. No more than twenty feet away stood a small but apparently angry stranger in black with a ski mask stretched over his head. Tara lunged forward, but he blocked her attack easily with a punch, and she fell to the floor, knocked out. The Fighter began to walk towards Lily, pulling a large net out of his pocket.

Lily desperately scanned her surroundings for a weapon. Tiles on the floor ... those were probably nailed in. Torches on the wall ... hmm ... Lily snatched a torch from a nearby holder.

The Fighter raised its net. Lily wielded the torch. The net was tossed. Lily threw the torch.

The net sailed through the air and Lily dodged, the trap clattering to the floor. The flaming torch brushed the Fighter's arm, but that was enough. The fire spread over the yelping attacker. The Fighter ran down the hall as fast as his little legs could carry him, away from Lily. Help arrived just in time to see a boot vanishing out of an open door.

Chapter 3

Training to fight

After the Fighter incident, both Jake and Tara insisted that Lily goes to the combat room to train. "Besides," Jake added. "We don't want you being attacked so many times. At least you should be able to defend yourself."

One trip to the P.O.O.P. and *voila*! Lily was in front of the combat room. Tara watched in silence as Jake led Lily through a small door.

There was nothing much to train with, just a human/elf-sized target and a table topped with assorted weapons. Lily picked up a dart gun. "Ah, the dart gun!" Jake exclaimed. "Only for emergencies, they are very easy to use. Just aim and shoot. No loading or cocking necessary." Whoosh! Lily managed to clip the shoulder of the target. She put the weapon down and picked up a human pistol, along with a bunch of ammo. "Where did you get this?" she asked. Jake didn't answer. Lily aimed the gun at the target and pulled the trigger. Nothing happened. Lily swore under her breath and loaded the gun.

BANG! The shock of the discharge traveled down Lily's arm, causing her to miss the target entirely. The bullet punched a hole in a wall. Jake coughed nervously. Lily tried again, cocking the gun and bracing her arm. This time, the bullet hit the target.

Lily set the pistol on the table and picked up a small grenade. Deciding not to ask Jake what the weapon was, she tossed it at the target.

ZAAAAAAAAAAPFWOOOOOM!! A bolt of crackling light shot out of the grenade and slammed into the target, setting the whole thing on fire. "Be careful!" Jake shrieked. "That's a *lightning bomb*!"

One hour later, Lily walked out of the combat room carrying a bag filled with one dart gun, the human pistol and fifteen lightning grenades plus ten explosive grenades and five sleep bombs. Tara looked at Lily's new bag. "Did Jake tell you about the ogre?" she asked. "What ogre?" Lily said. "Yes, the ogre!" Jake exclaimed. "I suppose you humans would call it that. I forgot! So, every combat trainee has to fight an ogre on their first day. You know, to test their skills. If the ogre likes you, maybe you don't have to fight it. And no, you may not kill the ogre." Lily shuddered at the thought of a friendly ogre prancing around her. She decided to keep that image to herself.

Soon Lily found herself in front of a giant room made of stone. Next to her, Tara smiled. "Don't worry," she said. "We'll be able to watch you from that window. She pointed to a small thick piece of glass secured in the stone. "Good luck!" Jake said. Lily took a deep breath and pushed open the door.

The inside of the room was littered with scraps of metal - the ogre's toys, perhaps. Lily faced a twelve-foot tall creature with large sandaled feet and an evil, hungry look on its face. The ogre wore nothing but a tattered loincloth. *Yuck.* Seriously, it was the 21st century.

It roared and slowly approached Lily. She rummaged around in her bag and grabbed an explosive grenade. Lily experimentally tossed it at the ogre's feet.

BOOM! The explosion was enough to send Lily tumbling across the floor and to knock the ogre off its feet. A dazed Lily managed to stand up while a very angry ogre ran towards her. "Uh, I don't think the ogre likes you!" Jake said. He had opened the window and was leaning through to get a better look. "I KNOW!" Lily yelled. The ogre roared and lobbed a clump of metal at Jake, who slammed the window shut just as it crashed into the thick glass, which cracked. The ogre now stood five feet in front of her. The creature slowly rose one sandaled foot. Lily's fingers closed around the dart gun. She aimed and fired a dart into the bottom of the big foot.

ROAAAAR! The foot came down and Lily rolled to one side. The ogre charged her again, but its movements were more sluggish. The ogre swung its arm at Lily, but the strike was ridiculously slow. Lily jumped over the arm and fired the dart gun three times, knocking out the ogre. The door opened. Jake and Tara rushed to meet Lily. "Congratulations!" Tara said. "You are now ready to fight just about anything that's really stupid." The words weren't very encouraging, but Lily smiled anyway.

Chapter 4

A war has begun

Two days later, the main elf city was overrun by little people. The warning came in the form of a bell ringing loudly. Lily scrambled out of bed. "Lily!" Jake stood at the doorway. "We need you downstairs, now!" Lily grabbed her bag of weapons and rushed out the door, Jake trailing behind. The alarm bell kept ringing, which was becoming *really* annoying. A crowd of elves surrounded the main city. The intruders shoved their way through, occasionally pausing to use their supply of sleep powder. Lily grabbed a random grenade from her bag, keeping her eyes on the enemy. The first attacker who emerged from the crowd hit Tara with a sleep bomb before she could punch him. She collapsed, unconscious. Lily threw the grenade.

ZAAAAAAAPFWOOM! Lily instantly knew something was wrong as lightning shot out of the grenade. She watched in fascinated horror as the writhing guy was enveloped in crackling light. The lightning dissipated and the attacker collapsed. The crowd gasped. The rest of the attackers immediately ran back the way they came. Jake ran to the person's side and checked his heartbeat. After a count of three, he stood up. "The attacker was a dwarf," he said. "By killing this intruder, we have destroyed our peace. A war has begun." *Oops.*

Even though Jake kept saying it wasn't Lily's fault, Lily could tell he was distressed. After Tara regained consciousness, she came to talk to Lily. "Lily," she said. "It's going to be okay. It's not entirely your fault.

We should've been more aware. The war can't be stopped, but we've found something that might help." Tara led Lily down several halls to a closed door. She knocked on the door. A woman with blond hair came out. "Lily, this is Stacy," Tara said. "She works in the control center. "Come in," Stacy said.

The control center was a replica of the NASA space center. There were just too many computers. The electronics crowded the room, filling the air with beeping sounds. Most of them had elves sitting in chairs, working. Stacy went to the nearest idle computer and plugged in a USB drive. "So," she said, typing furiously, "We are in a war with the dwarves. We have to create a powerful weapon to assist us in the battle. The problem is, we don't have a dwarf with us at the moment to test on and we need something with the same DNA. The only other beings with similar DNA are ..." Stacy spun the computer around to face Lily. She squinted at the picture. "A penguin?" "Exactly!" Stacy continued to type. Lily couldn't push away the thought that dwarves were related to penguins. "Your home planet, Earth, has no location that we know of with penguins. And becau..." Stacy continued.

"Stacy?"

"What?"

"What about Antarctica?"

Chapter 5

The South Pole

Lily never knew that the P.O.O.P. could take you anywhere in the universe.

As soon as she was bundled up, she went to the P.O.O.P. and got in the elevator box. She popped out of the container into Antarctica.

Wow. It felt so good to be back on her home planet, on the sort-of familiar ground. But now was not the time for daydreaming about New York City. She started to search the area, trudging through three-foot piles of snow and slipping on ice until she came upon a group of penguins. Lily was about to grab one when she remembered that Stacy had asked for a specific type of penguin. She knew these birds were definitely not Emperor penguins. Lily kept walking across the white landscape.

Lily nearly stepped on the next penguin.

She was about to trudge over a small heap of snow when the hill moved. Lily froze, her foot inches from an Emperor penguin. She put her foot down somewhere else and snatched the squawking bird up. Jogging back to the box, she jumped inside and traveled back to the elfin world (or as she called it: Planet Elf).

"You got the penguin!" Stacy snatched the bird out of Lily's arms. She jogged back to the control center, Lily trailing close behind. Stacy dropped the wiggling penguin in a glass box with a plastic penguin statue inside. Picking up a syringe, she injected a clear liquid into the bird's back before quickly closing the container. "Let's see if this works," Stacy said.

Seconds later the penguin began to writhe aggressively. Lily frowned. "Is it supposed to be like that?" "Yes," Stacy answered impatiently. "Now, shh!"

The bird slowly went back to normal. In a state of complete confusion but slight anger, the penguin turned to look at the statue. SQUAWK! The penguin attacked the figurine violently, kicking quite humorously with its feet and biting the plastic. "What is it doing?" Lily asked. "The wonders of liquid electronics," Stacy said proudly. "The affected dwarf should turn against its own species. I'll put the fluid in dart guns."

Chapter 6

Invasion of the dwarves

The day of the battle was a hustle of elves. The main city was crowded with elves as people rushed to get ready. Last week the walls had been heavily barricaded to keep out trespassers. Soldiers had slept next to the walls as a precaution.

Lily pulled a jacket over her t-shirt. She had been told to watch the battle from a safe distance inside her room. She was not to leave her living quarters unless absolutely necessary.

From a window, she could see a big army of dwarves approaching the walls, a massive blanket of tiny dots. Trumpets blew as elves, including Jake and Tara, ran to the end of the city, next to the northern wall. Everyone stood perfectly still, waiting for the war to begin.

BAM! Whoever was on the other side seemed to be using a battering ram to break through the north wall. To Lily, that was a terribly stupid idea; as the wall had a bigger chance to collapse and get a big gaping hole.

That was exactly what happened. As the dwarves' battering ram hit the wall one more time, the structure collapsed, causing utter chaos to both the elves and the dwarves as dust and debris filled the air. Elves stumbled around blindly. Dwarves dropped their weapons in surprise. Jake tripped over a rock and face-slammed the dirt. Back in her room,

Lily winced. Ouch. As the dust cleared, Lily began to see the thousands of dwarves that charged towards the elves.

Tara was one of the first elves to recover as she lobbed an explosive grenade into the dwarves' offensive line. KABOOM!! Little people flew everywhere. The elves seemed to be having the advantage in the war.

Suddenly a bright sphere appeared out of nowhere and hurtled towards the elves. Lily thought: *Why is the sun coming towards us?* Then she yelped and ducked as the sphere exploded.

Even though Lily's bedroom was a half mile away, the shockwave rattled the windows. The large pane of glass from which she watched the battle popped from its frame and fell to the ground, where it shattered. Tara was blown backward like a rag doll and crashed into another elf soldier. As the power of the blast hit Jake, he did an involuntary back flip and face-slammed the dirt even harder. Dazed, he staggered to his feet and yelled, "GAH!" as an airborne dwarf (was there such a thing as a flying dwarf?) landed on his head. Lily felt sorry for Jake. He was going to have plenty of bruises by the end of the battle.

Dwarves somehow managed to trample enemies into the dust despite their size as they advanced on the city. Tara hid behind a chunk of rubble from the wall. Lily had to do something, or the situation was going to get a lot worse. She grabbed her weapons bag and seizing five ultra-explosive grenades, yanked the window open and dropped them on the unsuspecting dwarf army.

BOOM! The detonation caused more dwarves to fly (whee) and took a big lump out of the ground. Lily could see Tara smacking her forehead in frustration. Below her, dozens of dwarves raised dart guns in Lily's direction. *Oh no*, she thought. *They were ready for that.* Lily swore and dropped to the ground as at least a hundred darts sailed through the large open window and over her head, embedding themselves in the wall behind her so it now resembled a flat silver porcupine.

Lily rolled to one side and ran out of her room, clutching her weapons bag. In the process, she pocketed one of her ultra-explosive grenades, just in case she lost her weapons bag. She lost her way and sped up a flight of stairs and suddenly found herself standing on a glass platform just above the nearest P.O.O.P. chute. Being so high up made Lily feel nauseous. She attached her weapons bag to her belt and crawled her way across the glass.

Creak. Lily's palm rested on a hinged glass door about halfway across the platform. She managed to kick it open. Her feet dangled above the P.O.O.P. elevator box. A dwarf stood with two other companions near the box, having a conversation. "-so what do you think the button does?" one asked. Another dwarf belched disgustingly. "I dunno," he said. "Let's find out!" With a hearty laugh, he slammed the transport button with his thumb. The container door slid open. *It's now or never,* Lily thought. Taking a deep breath she slid off the platform.

As she fell, Lily instantly found a reason why her plan would go terribly wrong. The drop was at least ten feet. Under her, there was no net, no cushions, no padding whatsoever. A bit of bad planning on her part.

Lily landed on a pile of packing boxes. The boxes cushioned her impact, but her fall had not gone unnoticed. The three dwarves spun around, guns at the ready. Lily flopped inside the metal box as darts hit the ground inches from her. As the door closed Lily used her pistol to shoot the transport button so the dwarves couldn't use it again.

Chapter 7

The *Alpha 201* lifts off

Stacy was beating up a computer.

Sometimes she thought that the control center had way too many computers. They blocked her way when she was in a hurry. Monitors on the floor tripped her at almost every step. Breaking one *could* create more space, but she almost never had that much steam to vent. Her fingers moved over a keyboard rapidly. The control center was empty for the moment, the elves on lunch break. She was trying to create a last minute weapon to save her friends and her people. So far, she wasn't having much luck.

Why couldn't things work out the way Stacy wanted it to be? She wished that she could just magically create something that could save the world. Unfortunately, things like that didn't come easily.

Those stupid dwarves had bypassed every single weapon the elves had at the moment. Their army had plowed through their army like a scissor on tissue paper. Now millions of elfin lives depended on Stacy and her knowledge. But technology could only go so far.

Stacy tried her last idea: to combine all the weapons into one super weapon. A notice on the computer told her that the weapons could not be put together, due to lack of dwarf DNA. She swore. "Dang it!" They had sent the penguin back to Earth just a day before. Stacy banged her fist on the laptop and it started to smoke. "Oh ... no, no, NO!" Stacy stomped her foot on the ground and yanked her USB out of the computer before it could be destroyed. Stacy stuffed the stick in her pocket.

She started to pace the room, passing laptops and bumping chairs. "What do I do? There's got to be something I can do," Stacy muttered. Her voice faltered as a crazy thought popped into her mind. "Oh ..."

The spaceship. She hadn't used it for decades (in fact, she hadn't used it at all), but there was a slim chance it could still fly. It was also big enough to hold at least fifty assorted weapons. Stacy loaded all the weaponry she could find in the control room onto a large cart and started to drag it to the garage where the plane was kept. To her, the plan was perfect! But it was a plane for two people: one to fly it, and one to handle the weapons inside. She *could* fly the spaceship, but she decided to handle the weaponry. Now all she needed was a pilot ...

Behind Stacy, a metal box appeared in the transport chute.

***

Lily squatted in the container, wondering where she was going. She hadn't entered a destination in advance, so the place where she ended up was random. Would she go back to Earth? Forget it! Would she pop up in the middle of the dwarf army? Most likely. The box door slid open and Lily climbed out, dreading the worst.

***

Stacy was so surprised *not* to see a dwarf coming out of the transport container she nearly fainted in relief. She was even happier to see Lily safe. "Lily!" she said. "Help me with this!" Lily stepped forward and took hold of the cart handle. "What are all these weapons for?" she asked. "Spaceship," Stacy said. Lily blinked. "Excuse me?" Stacy explained to her about the plane and what she was about to do. Lily said, "No offense, Stacy, but what chance do we have that the spaceship can still fly?" "It's the best chance we've got," Stacy said. "This idea is absolutely bonkers," Lily warned. "I know," she replied, pushing open the garage door.

The spaceship nearly took Lily's breath away.

The whole thing was designed for combat. She could tell from the sleekness of the plane. The words Alpha 201 gleamed in gold on one side. "This is the Alpha 201," Stacy said proudly. "I built it all by myself." With that, she dragged the cart to the plane and opened a hatch on the bottom. Carefully loading the weapons in the plane, Stacy gestured for Lily to get in.

Lily entered through the place where countless weapons were stored and walked to the cockpit. The door creaked behind her as Stacy shut the compartment. "Who's flying the spaceship?" Lily asked. "You are," Stacy said. "What?" Stacy joined Lily in the cockpit. "I'm the only person who knows how to operate every single one of the weapons," she said. Lily strapped herself into the pilot's seat as Stacy opened the garage door with the touch of a button and gave her instructions. "Listen," she said. "That lever makes the aircraft fly up and down -" Lily yanked the handle back and the spaceship shot up, knocking her to the ground. Luckily, the ceiling was high.

Stacy peeled herself off the floor. "That hurt," she groaned. "Anyway, that lever makes the aircraft go forward and backward. Don't pull it too hard or-" The spaceship lurched forward. They were now at least two hundred feet away from the garage. "Careful!" Stacy yelled. "Last instruction: the joystick makes the aircraft turn left or right." Lily wiggled the joystick gently and the spaceship twisted to the right. "Actually ..." Stacy said. "Maybe I should fly this thing."

Stacy guided the plane to the nearest dwarf group, which was just outside the western tower. Lily grabbed a grenade gun and opened a window. "Hey!" she yelled. "Catch this, you stupid dwarves!" A touch-activated bomb shot out of the gun barrel and a dwarf instinctively caught it.

KABOOM! The grenade exploded in a plume of fire. The plane was gone before the smoke cleared. "Great!" Stacy said. "One group of dwarves down, only about a gazillion more to go!"

***

Jake despised dwarves.

Because of those danged little people, his face had been slammed into the dirt twice and trampled into the dust. He could drop kick every single one of them, but unfortunately, he didn't know where they were. Groaning, Jake sat up and wiped the dirt off his face. His head ached and he was bruised all over the place. There was no sign of Tara. Jake stood up and managed to stagger to the western wall, where he could find help. He turned a corner and nearly bumped into a dwarf.

Jake froze and inched back around the corner. Luckily, the group of dwarves had their backs turned, gaping up at the sky as a spaceship came into view. Jake looked up in amazement. Was that Stacy in the cockpit? As he watched, a window on the side popped open and Lily's head poked out. "Hey!" she yelled. "Catch this, you stupid dwarves!" She pointed a gun through the window and fired a grenade. A dwarf caught it. "Crap!" Jake muttered. The bomb exploded in a massive fireball as he dove for cover.

Coughing, Jake climbed to his feet. The spaceship had disappeared. Jake waved the smoke away from his face. All the dwarves were flat on the ground unconscious, except for one, who was stumbling dizzily around and calling for help. Jake stepped forward and punched him in the face. The dwarf collapsed, joining his comrades on the ground. Jake, satisfied with his work, jogged to the tower door.

Chapter 8

Fire!

In one hour the Alpha 201 had destroyed more than fifty groups of dwarves, thanks to Lily and her dangerous array of weapons. She had to be careful, though. One mistake or one wrong throw, and the impressive elfin city below them could go BOOM!

Stacy landed the spaceship next to the east tower door. Lily jumped out of the aircraft and raced through the tower entrance, a grenade at the ready. She sped past the now obliterated infirmary, leaped over a flight of stairs, turned a corner and crashed into Tara.

Lily and Tara fell over as they slammed into each other. "Tara!" Lily gasped. "What are you doing here?" "I escaped," Tara replied, which pretty much summed up everything. "We need to go through that doorway!" Stacy shouted, pointing at an open door behind Tara. "Yeah, but-" Lily looked over Tara's shoulder. "Dwarf!"

The dwarf must have been patrolling the hallways and as he came into view, he yelled, "Hey!" and pulled out a dart gun. "Go!" Tara commanded and leaped forward. Lily and Stacy sprinted through the door as Tara performed a professional headlock on the dwarf. Lily turned back. "Tara!" she yelled. "Come with us!" "Not enough time!" Tara replied. "Now, GO!"

Lily and Stacy ran through a deserted corridor, leaping over rubble and ducking under broken metal beams. "Are you sure where we're going?" Lily said between gasps of breath. "Absolutely *not*!" Stacy replied. The tunnel opened into the P.O.O.P. The metal transport container was now missing from the chute. Maybe Lily shouldn't have shot that button. "What's the fastest way to the building roof?" she asked. "The P.O.O.P.," Stacy said. "But the box is gone and the button's destroyed." Lily did some quick thinking for a few moments. "The transportation," she said. "How does it work?" "Well," Stacy said, "first you enter your destination and press the button. You get in the box and-" "No, I already know that, but what does the box move on?" "Elevator cables, of course." "Elevator cables!" Lily exclaimed. She turned to Stacy. "I have the craziest idea ever but I don't have time to tell you right now," she said.

Lily ran to the empty box pit and looked down. Sure enough, thick cables dangled down the dark tunnel. Maybe she should tell Stacy what this was all about. "I'm going to jump," she said. "Don't you d - Lily!" Stacy yelled.

Lily had jumped into the hole and was now clinging to one of the cables. Stacy was about to jump in after Lily when she stopped her. "Meet me at the south tower next to the nearest transport tunnel," she said. After a moment's silence, she added, "Well, what are you waiting for? Go!" A reluctant Stacy ran out a random door.

Ten seconds later, Lily punched the air in frustration and started to fall, grabbing the cable just in time. *Stupid idea*! She thought. How would she even *find* the southern tower? But Stacy had already left, so there was no other choice but to move on. Lily took a deep breath and carefully shinnied down the wire.

Soon Lily faced an intersection, with wires going left and right. There were multiple steel cables lined up side by side. Above Lily, the wire began to groan and break. The cables to the left had fallen from their supports. She twisted to the right. The gap between the two wires was at least five feet. She swung back and forth to gather momentum and launched herself from the wire.

Her fingers brushed the wire, grabbing thin air. Lily yelped as her left hand dangled in the dim blackness. She lunged for the cable and managed to wrap it around her right hand. She hung on for dear life, trying to reach the wire with her other hand.

Success! Lily now gripped the thick wire with both hands. She began the journey through the elevator chute.

Lily finally saw a rectangle-shaped opening above her. Light streamed through the gap. She pulled herself up and lay gasping for breath on the floor. A voice behind her said, “Lily?” “Stacy,” Lily croaked, “Help me up.” A hand roughly yanked her into a standing position. “Lily Claire,” Stacy said. “That was without a doubt the *dumbest* thing I’ve ever seen anyone do, and I *really* don’t like people who do dumb things.” “Uh ... sorry?” “Apology *not* accepted.”

Suddenly a roaring sound shook the ground. Lily and Stacy dashed to the nearest window. A wave of flaming arrows set the ground ablaze, the wall of flames speeding towards the elfin city. “The dwarves have not called the war their victory yet,” Stacy gasped. “They are well known for their fire weapons.” “Won’t the walls keep the fire out?” Lily asked. “Maybe.” It was then that Lily remembered the north wall had collapsed.

The sound of screaming broke through the air. Lily turned around. “What was that?” Behind her, Stacy shrieked. Lily whipped around to find that giant fireballs were sailing over the walls, devastating the main city. Buildings, big and small, were set ablaze. Elves ran around, screaming in terror. FWOOM! Lily looked up. "What the-"

KABLAAMOBOOM! An unnaturally big fireball crashed through the wall. Lily and Stacy were blown backward. Stacy tumbled across the floor, into a pile of packing boxes. Lily was not so lucky. She flew twenty feet into a hard stone wall. "OW!" she groaned. Stacy sat up, dazed. Her eyes were crossed, which might have been funny if it wasn't because a humongous ball of fire had punched a smoldering hole in the wall fifteen feet from her. Stacy staggered over to her side. "Are you all right?" she asked. "If someone has been blasted twenty feet into a wall, how could they be okay?" Lily said. Stacy didn't answer that.

Chapter 9

Over the hill and into the water

Tara hated to be alone.

But even as she ordered Lily to follow Stacy through the door without her, she knew it was the right choice. Now she couldn't have been less alone in her life - surrounded by dwarves.

The dwarves had appeared out of nowhere. The little people surrounded her in a loose semicircle, their weapons gleaming. Tara began to think fast. If she moved, they would knock her out with a dart or worse. If she stayed still, the dwarves would capture her anyway. A smart person wouldn't move.

Tara moved.

She leaped at the nearest dwarf and grabbing his wrist, flipped him to the ground. She ducked and rolled as grenades were thrown over her head. Tara ran as bombs burst on the floor inches away.

Uh oh, Tara thought as she began to tire. Those sleep bombs were easy enough to make anyone go *good night*. If she could make it to that door ...

The entrance to one of the countless hallways in the tower was fifty feet away ... forty feet away ... twenty feet away ... She dove for the door as a sleep grenade spilled its contents on her head. Dang it!

Chapter 9: Over the hill and into the water

***

Lily winced as she limped along the hard floor, leaning on Stacy's shoulder. That stupid fireball had blown her into the wall hard. She managed to stagger to the door. Stacy looked outside and frowned. "That's strange," she said. "The dwarves have disappeared." It was true. There was not a single dwarf in sight. "Let's check outside the wall," Lily suggested. Together they stumbled past the remains of the north wall and over a hill. "They're over there," Lily said, pointing.

Next to a lake, the remaining dwarves floated inside a giant pool of water, relaxing. Their location puzzled Lily. Why didn't they just swim in the lake? Lily's hand reached into her battered weapons bag. Her dart gun was gone, but at least she had a few grenades.

Lily pulled out a lightning bomb and lobbed it at the pool of water. ZAAAAAAAPFWOOOM! Light crackled through the ball of water and the dwarves inside went limp. The whole thing happened in five seconds, less than Lily expected, but water *is* an excellent conductor of electricity. The two walked down the hill.

No sooner than Lily's foot touched the bottom of the hill a growling sound echoed through the air. "Get down!" Lily hissed. As they crouched on the grass a sleep grenade exploded next to Stacy and she fell over. Lily scrambled to her side.

Thump. Lily glanced to her right to find a strange-looking bomb with a ticking timer on it.

3:00.

2:59.

Chapter 10

The bomb

Lily started to stand up but a voice interrupted her. "I wouldn't move a single bit, Lily!" A dwarf stood on the top of the hill, smiling. "There are sensors on the bomb to detect air movements." "What about her?" Lily asked, pointing to Stacy. "Oh, don't worry!" the dwarf smiled. "I've set the grenade to target you and *only* you. Nobody else will be affected."

2:27.

2:26.

Lily tried to act calm. "Why haven't you detonated the bomb now, huh?" she called. "Too scared?" The dwarf scowled. "How ... how dare you!" he sputtered. "Nobody speaks to me like that!"

1:59.

1:58.

Lily kept talking. "So you think you've won the war? You're wrong. The elves have countless weapons in stock for you." The dwarf snorted. "Untrue!" he yelled. "Yes, true!" Lily yelled back. "You have a good imagination, human," the dwarf seethed. "But we have already won."

1:00.

0:59.

Chapter 10: The bomb

Talking wasn't going to do any good. Unless Lily could trick the dwarf ...

"Look! A giant booger!" she screamed.

Apparently, the dwarf knew what a giant booger was because he whipped around in terror. When he saw nothing, he laughed. "A good try," he admitted, "but if you think you're going to escape, forget it. For I am Alban the dwarf, and no one has ever escaped my wrath."

0:17.

0:16.

Lily had to do something fast, or the bomb would explode. She did have some advantages, though. She was quicker and taller than the dwarf, and she was completely out of her mind. "Alban, you're scared of giant boogers, and you think you still can catch me?" she laughed. Lily dropped to the ground and rolled to the big lake. BOOM! The grenade exploded in a shockwave of barbed wire, but the force of the shockwave hit Lily's back, ten feet away. Instead of being destroyed, the powerful blast only gave more momentum to Lily's roll. Her jacket, which already had holes in it from the barbed wire, ripped on a sharp rock as she passed it. As she dropped to the water, Lily could hear Alban howling in rage as an elf attacked him from behind.

She swam as fast as she could, not daring to look back as the strong current sped her on her way. *Bong!* The sound was like a muffled explosion as Lily banged her shoulder against a metal wall. She looked and saw a circular door made of glass set in the metal. A tunnel stretched behind it. Lily yanked at the handle. The door didn't budge. She began to panic. Her air was running out and returning to the surface was risking capture. Lily pulled her legs all the way back, slamming them into the door. Nothing happened. She tried again. A spider web of cracks appeared on the door. She kicked at the door a third time, and the glass shattered. A new current quickly sucked Lily through the new opening, the broken glass scratching at her arms.

Lily bumped against the tunnel wall as she was roughly pushed forward by the current. Her strength was mostly spent from swimming around and kicking the door. Even worse, her lungs were crying out for air. Lily had to resist the urge to open her mouth for oxygen that wouldn't be there.

The water spat her out into another deep pool of water. *Not more water*, Lily thought. If she ever got through this, she wasn't going to the beach for a long time. Above her sunlight rippled through the dim blue-gray liquid. She used the last of her strength to kick upwards.

Lily gasped for air as her head emerged from the surface of the water. Pulling herself onto shore, Lily filled her lungs with unbelievable amounts of air. After five minutes of gasping and wheezing, she managed to stand up. Her sodden clothes dripped with water. Lily stumbled to the nearest rock and sat on it. As she tried to shake the water out of her hair Lily wondered where her friends were.

***

Stacy woke up sprawled on the grass. Groaning, she flopped over in different directions, trying to locate Lily. She was sure that she was standing next to her only a few seconds ago. As Stacy climbed to her feet she saw a burst grenade shell on the ground with several particles of sleep powder inside. "I knew it!" she said. But why was there a second grenade shell next to it? Stacy crouched down to take a closer look. She squinted at the weapon code. *4798173E*, the label read. It was an explosive bomb. The empty shells rolled around as wind ruffled Stacy's hair. Something smacked into her face. Her fingers closed around a piece of cloth. "What the-" Stacy recognized the jagged fabric from Lily's black jacket. Lily was most definitely in trouble. Clutching the cloth, Stacy jogged back to the elf city.

The main city was packed with elf soldiers and dwarves, creating an action-packed scene of violence. "Go away, you fat little fiends!" Jake yelled as he kicked a dwarf in his little butt. Another dwarf clung to his back like a baby, screaming as he was shaken around vigorously. Stuffing the cloth in her pocket, Stacy joined the fight.

Chapter 11

Outnumbered

"She is a good little elf, don't you think?" "Absolutely. The girl will make a nice servant for us dwarves!" Tara woke up, startled. The voices belonged to dwarves, no doubt about that. She was shocked at their plans. Servant for the dwarves? What were they *thinking*?

Tara was loosely tied to a post only by her hands. Her captors were either inexperienced or total idiots. Slowly, careful not to cause any suspicion, she put all her weight onto the post and kicked forward.

Both of Tara's feet slammed into the dwarves and they fell backward with a yell of surprise. She opened her eyes and wriggled out of her bonds. The dwarves lay on the ground, groaning. Tara stepped over them without a glance and searched for the nearest exit.

***

Lily reached the east tower ... or what was left of it. Half of the tower had collapsed into piles of rubble and dust. She found a ladder behind a chunk of stone. The metal rungs stretched up to the roof. Lily put her foot on a rung and began to climb.

Lily soaked clothes dripped water as she slowly made her way up the ladder. She was tired, but she kept her mind on climbing. Lily kept thinking: *So you put one foot up and then one hand up and repeat to climb the ladder*. After what felt like hours, she reached the tower roof.

Chapter 11: Outnumbered

Exhausted, Lily dragged herself up onto the cold stone floor. In front of her was a cabin with a closed door. If she could get to that door, she could find help. Lily rose to her feet and managed to stagger to the door, pushing it open.

Lily's surroundings were covered in darkness, so she didn't see the set of stairs in front of her. With a loud THUMP, Lily tripped and fell down the stairs. "Ow!" She felt her way up another small flight of stairs and ended up on what seemed to be a walkway. Lily rested her hand on a wall and accidentally flipped a switch.

Lily was momentarily blinded as light flooded the walkway. She blinked. There was no walkway in front of her. Instead, open air stood between her and another building roof fifteen feet below her. Lily swore and turned to go back. A rumbling sound broke through the air, heading rapidly towards her. A fireball sped towards the tower. Lily groaned as she realized what she had to do. She turned and jumped off the roof as the tower exploded behind her in a ball of fire.

Lily hit the other building roof running as she fled from the flying debris. Her heart beat rapidly as she sprinted away. Every now and then, a piece of rubble would fly past her face and crack the floor in front of her. Lily sprinted down a hallway. As she headed deeper into the building, she wondered where everyone else was.

Crack! The floor in front of Lily caved in. Too late to stop, she fell through the hole. Luckily, the ground was only five feet below Lily. As she got up, she could hear the sounds of fighting. Lily ran outside towards the noise.

"Aieeeeee!" A dwarf screamed as he sailed through the air, nearly smacking Lily in the face. A roar of battle shook the towers. Lily could see Jake yelling like a madman as he kicked and punched his way through a crowd of dwarves. Stacy was wrestling with a fat dwarf. Tara was nowhere to be seen.

Lily saw all of this with one worried thought in her mind. There were *much* more dwarves than elves. When one dwarf went down, two more took his place. If Lily joined the fight, what help would she be? But she could still fight. Lily yelled in defiance and jumped into battle.

Lily leaped onto an unsuspecting dwarf and he fell over with a squeal of terror. As she kicked another dwarf in the butt, she heard a strange whistling sound. Lily looked up.

KABOOOOM! A shockwave blasted everyone backward in a shockwave of hot air. Lily tumbled over the ground, coming to rest on top of a piece of rock. She gasped for air but there was nothing to inhale but pure heat. As the smoke cleared, disoriented elves and dwarves alike stumbled around. Lily found Jake sprawled on the ground and helped him to his feet. "Tara, is that you?" he asked. His eyes widened as the last wisps of smoke drifted away. "Lily!" he gasped. "What are you doing here? I thought you were in your room!" "I changed the plan," Lily replied. She ran into the dwarf crowd before Jake could argue.

Chapter 12

Dwarves are really stupid

Lily wasn't in the mood to fight.

She was tired, hungry, thirsty, and a bunch of other things. Lily stumbled through the crowd of dwarves, punching them with a tired but determined shout. As she raised her fist to hit another dwarf, a single small bomb sailed through the air and rolled to a stop right in front of her. As Lily opened her mouth to scream, the bomb exploded and she flew backward into the battling crowd. She yelled "OW!" as she slammed against someone, falling in a heap to the floor. The person scrambled off her. "Lily?"

"Stacy!" Lily said. "Where have you been?" Stacy demanded. Lily didn't answer, probably because she was looking over Stacy's shoulder at the giant grenade hurtling towards them.

KABOOM! The bomb exploded in a burst of glittering powder. All around Lily, dwarves put on gas masks. She just had time to think *sleep powder* before she drifted into unconsciousness.

***

Tara was *not* having a good day.

Of course, what would you expect from someone when she was captured by some dwarves with a war going on? But at least Tara escaped. So now her main priority was to find an exit, get out of wherever she was, and hopefully send some dwarves crying for their mommas.

She was *not* in the elfin city. The elf buildings didn't have hallways with little to no doors. Tara jumped a flight of stairs and came to a door. *Finally*, she thought as she pushed it open.

"Hey! Who are you?" Tara faced a group of dwarves surrounding a table. The leader began to approach her. "Bye!" Tara quickly backed out of the doorway and sprinted down the hall. The yells of "Get her!" and "Catch that woman!" filled the hall as Tara raced down the path. She pushed at the nearest door and the rusted lock crumbled into dust. The door creaked, but it didn't budge. Tara swore and shoved the door open. Fresh air flooded the room and Tara dashed out onto the grass, closing the door behind her. She sighed in relief.

Bang! The door crashed open and the dwarves rushed out, forming a loose semi-circle around Tara. The leader smiled coldly. "There's no place to run now," he said. The dwarf turned to his comrades. "Get her!"

The first attacker ran towards Tara and she grabbed his wrist, flipping him onto his back. Before more dwarves could follow, she charged the leader. The dwarf's eyes widened as Tara captured him in a headlock. The other dwarves froze nervously. "Let him go!" one yelled. "Not happening," Tara said. The dwarves waited for her to release their leader. She sighed. Were they really so dumb? "Whatever," she said, dropping the headlock. The dwarf jumped to his feet and scrambled to safety. The rest of the dwarves advanced towards Tara. As she prepared to fight, she spotted the elves' west tower not too far away.

Chapter 12: Dwarves are really stupid

The west tower! If Tara could get there, then she could get help. She wasn't doomed after all. She thought of a way to defeat the dwarves. They were skilled in fighting, that was for sure. Fortunately, they were also very, very short, and they were easily scared.

"BOOGERS!" she yelled. The dwarves froze in surprise and looked around in terror. Tara dashed around them and ran for the tower.

She shoved the tower door open and ran as fast as she could to the control center. Opening a garage Tara entered to find it was empty. "Dang it!" she said. Running to the other garage, Tara found a brand-new spaceship for emergencies. The situation she had in mind was definitely an emergency.

Chapter 13

The war goes on

SWOOP! Lily woke up. What was causing that sound? Turning around she saw an elfin spaceship hovering above the battle scene. A large tube jutted out of the bottom and it seemed to be sucking up all the dwarves. When the last dwarf disappeared into the tube, a glass sphere attached to the back of the aircraft filled to the brim with dwarves. With a loud BANG, the sphere launched into the distance. The side cockpit window popped open and Tara's face poked out. "Tara!" Lily yelled. "Tara?" Stacy said, causing Lily to jump. She hadn't realized Stacy had woken up yet. As the spaceship landed other elves began to stir. Tara jumped out of the spaceship and ran to meet Lily. "Is that my spaceship?" Stacy asked. "We won the battle!" Lily said with delight. "Not yet," Tara said. "Come." As Lily followed her into the west tower Stacy said, "You have no idea what a war is."

Tara led Lily and Stacy into the control center. Stacy ran to one of her precious computers as Lily and Tara sat down in some chairs. "If one side wins a war," Stacy explained, "The losing side will want revenge, possibly starting another war," "So ..." Lily said. "There's going to be another war?" "Most likely," Tara replied.

Lily wailed in distress. "Another war?" she cried. "Why?" "You know perfectly well why." Stacy didn't take her eyes off the computer. "We're wasting time." The three crowded around the computer as Stacy typed. "It's almost certain that the dwarves will start another battle, probably with double as much fighters as last time, so we need to create something twice as powerful as our latest technology," she said. "Like ... what, exactly?" Lily asked. "Follow me," Stacy said as she walked to a door.

Inside the room, there was one empty table and another three tables with random weapons and labeled glass vials. "Where are we?" Tara asked. Even she didn't know about the room. Stacy didn't answer. She was too busy putting on a lab coat and a pair of rubber gloves. Stacy snatched a vial from a table. Pouring some of the stuff into a Petri dish she slid it under a microscope. After a few moments of looking, Stacy snapped her fingers at Lily. "Get the vial labeled iodine dioxide," she ordered.

For hour after hour, Stacy pummeled Lily and Tara with instructions. Lily watched in fascination as the liquid in the Petri dish changed from brown to purple to neon pink. As Stacy added the final ingredient to the liquid, a roar of an angry crowd shook the ground. Tara ran to the window and gasped. Lily peered out of the glass. Over the hill, beyond the wall, a large ... no, *humongous* carpet of dwarves marched towards the elfin city. It would be just like the previous war, with an overwhelming number of dwarves. Only this time, there would be no walls to stop them from charging straight into the elfin city.

Lily managed to take her eyes away from the monstrous sight, rushing to the table where Stacy was working. "We've got company! You need to hurry!" Lily said. "Hold on!" Stacy said as she poured the now bright purple liquid into unused grenade shells. "These might not work," Stacy said. "But it's the best chance we've got." The three stuffed as many grenades as possible into plastic bags they found on the floor and ran out of the room.

As Lily sprinted down a hall Stacy explained to her and Tara how the grenades worked. "To detonate the bomb there's a red button you can't miss that activates a five-second timer. Press the button, toss the grenade at the enemy and get out of the area as fast as possible," she said. "Got it," Lily said.

Lily, Stacy and Tara burst out of the northern door. The dwarf army had reached the city and was now climbing over chunks of rubble. "Any last words before we kick some dwarf bottoms?" Tara asked. "I hate dwarves," Lily said. "I am so ready to beat up those dwarves," Stacy added. They yelled in defiance and charged into battle.

Chapter 14

A stupid idea

As soon as Lily started punching dwarves, several shapes appeared on the top of the hill. As they got closer Lily's puzzlement turned to dread. Tara swore. "Ogres," she said. Stacy, who tended to be on the obvious side of things, said, "Oh, that's not good." The ogres roared and lumbered towards the battle scene. "Whose side are they on?" Lily asked. "Definitely the dwarves," Tara replied. Lily's fingers tightened around her grenade bag. "I'm going up there," she said. Tara and Stacy stared at her in shock. "Are you serious?" Tara asked. "You're going to get yourself killed!" Stacy said. Lily nodded in agreement and pushed her way through the dwarf crowd.

There were too many dwarves.

The small people were so large in quantity and so packed together that it was almost impossible to get to the ogres. But Lily still managed to reach the bottom of the hill. She opened her bag and pulled a grenade out. She pressed her thumb into the detonation button and lobbed the bomb at the ogres. As soon as the grenade had left her hand, Lily turned and ran as fast as she could. But even though she was fast, she wasn't fast enough.

KABOOM! The bomb exploded in a massive shockwave, throwing Lily fifty feet backward into the grass. Groaning, she looked up to find a massive cloud of stars flying up into the air. As they descended, they turned into powder.

A few grains of the dust drifted onto Lily's arm. She winced as the powder touched her skin, becoming tiny, searing stabs of pain. Where the particles made contact with her skin, they left angry red marks. It was even worse for the ogres. The majority of the powder had fallen all over the giant creatures. They roared in pain, clawing at their eyes and scratching at their skin. After what seemed like forever, the ogres raised their heads. Their eyes were red and teary.

ROAARRR! The ogres charged down the hill. The grenades Stacy had created hadn't worked well enough to keep them away. Lily gasped in terror and fled, shoving dwarves out of her way as they were trampled underfoot by the ogres. She reached Tara and Stacy. Stacy grabbed Lily's arm. "Well, the grenade worked," she noted. "Not well enough," Lily replied. "RUN!" Tara screamed as the ogres charged at them. They dove out of the way as the giant creatures cracked the ground where they were just standing. Lily watched as the ogres charged past. Unfortunately, you couldn't get away that easily if you throw a lethal grenade at someone.

The ogres turned towards Lily. Apparently, they recognized her as the puny girl who gave them the biggest skin rash of their lives. Growling, the ogres ran at her. "I think running would be a really good idea right now," Lily said. "I'll go get some help from the other soldiers," Stacy suggested. "Me too," Tara said. Lily pressed her grenade bag into Stacy's hands and ran.

As Lily's feet pounded the ground, the rumbling of ogre's feet could be heard behind her. She shoved dwarves out of her way, leaping over rocks and the occasional very tiny dwarf. Dwarves and elves screamed at the sight of the horrendous monsters hurtling at them. Lily jumped over another rock, burst through the northern tower door and slammed it closed.

Lily ran to the nearest window and looked through it. The group of ogres had paused in front of the door, searching and sniffing for their prey. A trail of squashed dwarves (the elves managed to jump out of the way just in time) lay in their wake. An ogre turned its head and Lily quickly ducked out of sight. But it was too late. The ogre had seen her.

ROAR!! The wall in front of Lily exploded into piles of rocks and debris and she tumbled across the floor. She dragged herself, coughing, behind a stone pillar. Lily sneaked a glance around the pillar and was amazed to find that only one ogre stood in the piles of rubble. The others had probably gone to search for her somewhere else. The ogre lumbered towards the pillar, crushing rocks underfoot.

A panicked Lily looked around for a way to escape. There were several hallways, but they were too far away. A door stood twenty feet away from Lily, but the ogre was right next to it, so that wasn't an option.

That left the P.O.O.P. chute. It was in the ogre's line of sight, so it was impossible to get there unseen. But it was also the best chance Lily had. She made up her mind and ran for the chute.

The ogre spotted her immediately. Roaring, it charged her, the fangs in its mouth gleaming. Lily reached the transport hole and as she suspected, there was no elevator box. It would be too slow, anyway. Lily jumped in as one of the ogre's feet stomped the ground where she was standing before.

Lily was in free-fall.

She knew if she grabbed on to a cable, she was risking getting caught by the ogre. Through the dim light, she saw a large hand go through the hole towards her. *Uh oh*, she thought. A cable intersection was below her. That meant she had about twenty seconds or so to either grab the cable or plummet into who-knows-where. The end of the cable was about fifteen feet below her.

Lily gritted her teeth to prevent her from howling in frustration. What should she do? What was the best choice?

At the last second, Lily stretched her arms out and wrapped her hands around the cable. Success!

The ogre's fingers closed an inch from Lily. Unfortunately, the ogre's sharp fingernails also severed the cable Lily was holding on to. Definitely *not* a success.

Chapter 15

Journey in the chute

As Lily plummeted down into the darkness, she wondered why ogres hated elves in the first place. Then she thought, *Of course! The elves have used ogres for combat training for years! Why did they do that in the first place?*

CREEEAAAK! Lily hit a thick line. Her hand brushed against a cable … .a cable!

Lily looked more closely at her arms and legs through the dim light. Sure enough, she was snagged on several of the thick wires. She was just about to start climbing when a screeching sound interrupted her. A cable next to her sizzled and smoked as electricity pass through it.

Lily's mind screamed in frustration. How was she supposed to climb her way up *now*? Were there other handholds? Lily kicked forward with her legs into empty space. Nope. She swung away from the damaged cable to a sturdy one and waited until the wire had completely broken off before she continued on.

***

As it turned out, Tara and Stacy could *not* find help, and they wasted valuable time trying.

Apparently, all the other elves had joined the elf/dwarf war. As the two approached the battle scene, Tara frowned. "Hmm," she said. "We seem to be at an impasse with the war." Stacy looked around and saw it was true. The dwarves had recovered and they didn't seem to be losing, but they didn't seem to be winning either. It was the same with the elves. "Well then," she said. "I suppose we'll have to join the fight." They ran into the crowd, fists flying.

While Tara kicked dwarf butt, Stacy spotted a group of thirteen dwarves climbing over what was left of the northern tower wall. Without a moment's hesitation, she followed them.

After five minutes of walking and opening doors, the dwarves came to a stop. They entered a conference room with a table and several chairs. The dwarves took a seat.

"Welcome to the elf building!" one dwarf said. He jumped out of his seat. Making points over his ears with his hands, he did a mock bow. The dwarf's friends laughed delightfully. He sat down again. "Now," he said, "We need to find the elves' ultimate weapon. Think for a moment. What will the elves throw at us? Candy ants?" The other dwarves doubled over with laughter. *I'll give you an ultimate weapon,* Stacy thought. Quickly, she took five itch grenades from Lily's bomb bag. Pressing the detonation buttons, she hurled them in the room and closed the door before sprinting down the hallway.

KABOOM! The explosion rattled the walls. Stacy was literally lifted off her feet by the shockwave, sending her sprawling at the end of the hallway. Even from fifty feet away, she could hear the dwarves' wails as the skin rash powder came down on them. *Another victory for the elves,* Stacy thought.

Chapter 16

Whee

Lily was hungry.

How many hours had it been since she'd eaten? Four hours? Five hours? Lily's stomach growled loudly as she shinnied up the long cable. The darkness stretched on for eternity.

Lily was starting to think that she was going to be trapped down here forever when the darkness around her lessened, just a bit. Excited, she climbed up until her head poked out of a transport chute.

Tired and hungry, Lily pulled herself out of the hole. She seemed to be in the same cavernous room where Jake had told her about the elves when she had first arrived in the elfin world. She trudged on, feeling very much alone.

***

Tara was tired of kicking dwarf butt.

A drink would be nice. Finding Lily would be even better. But she couldn't leave that easily. Unless Lily was somewhere in the building ...

Tara punched another dwarf and ran to the northern tower rubble. Climbing over the pieces of rock, she sprinted down a random hallway, passing one of over 50 cafeterias in the building. She grabbed two apples and continued, crunching down one on the way. Five minutes later, she turned a corner and sprinted straight into Stacy.

"Why are you here?" Tara asked. "Those itch grenades work really well on dwarves," Stacy replied. As if on cue, several screams issued from behind a closed door. Tara nodded her approval and handed the second apple to Stacy. "All right," she said. "Let's go find Lily."

Stacy and Tara wandered down random hallways, calling for Lily. No one answered. They were just about to give up when a voice yelled, "Tara? Stacy? Anybody? Hello?"

"Lily!" Tara yelled. Footsteps clattered towards Tara and Stacy from another hallway. After two minutes Lily emerged from the entrance. "Hi," she said, breathlessly.

Stacy smiled and gave Lily her grenade bag, along with her uneaten apple. "Glad to have you back. Now, how do we win this war?" Tara pointed at a hallway. "Down there," she said.

Tara led Lily and Stacy to a closed door. She pushed it open, revealing a winding staircase and a long slide. Lily began to walk down the stairs but Tara stopped her. "Do you hear that?" A series of yells and loud footsteps echoed up the stairs. "A group of dwarves will be here any second," Stacy said. "So we go down the slide?" Lily asked. "Exactly," Tara replied. "But we will be too slow, so we do this." She reached over and pressed a hidden button.

FWOOSH! Holes on both sides of the slide opened, water rushing out. Tara jumped on with a gleeful laugh and disappeared down the slide. Stacy turned to Lily. "After you," she said. Lily jumped on was without a doubt the most dangerous water slide in the multi-universe.

Chapter 16: Whee

The water slide corkscrewed downward into a dim tunnel. The only sounds were that of rushing water, Lily's yelling of "WHEE!" and Stacy's screaming of "We're going to *dieeeee*!". A wave of water splashed over Lily's head and she resurfaced sputtering and spitting water.

The slide spat Lily, Tara and Stacy out on a stone ground. Dripping wet, they stood up. "Uh ... where are we?" Lily asked. A long corridor stretched out in front of them, illuminated by a few torches. "The elves' biggest secret," Tara said. "Follow me."

Chapter 17

The NPSbot (Nitrogen Powered Super-speed bot)

"Wow," Lily said. "Where are we?"

Stacy, Lily and Tara had entered a humongous chamber. Inside stood a robot the size of a three-story building, complete with mechanical hands and legs. The robot glowered at Lily. Instead of eyes, a window similar to a helmet visor was in its place. "This," Tara said proudly, "Is the NPSbot, also known as the Nitrogen Powered Super-speed bot. We call her Sally. We had one other robot named Carl, but he disappeared twenty years ago." Tara pointed at Sally. "Let's go."

The three entered the robot through her right leg, climbing a set of stairs until they reached the cockpit, which turned out to be the head of the robot. Lily looked at the controls, or rather, the *lack* of controls. "How does Sally work?" she asked. Tara gave her a helmet. "Put this on," she said. Lily pulled the helmet over her head and the visor lit up with images and words. She read the light instructions. *Okay,* she thought, *to walk say, "Commence walk". Any movement of the pilot (me) causes the robot to move in the same way. To use a weapon, a list will pop up in my visor. If I'm done reading, say "Instructions dismissed."*

"Instructions dismissed," Lily said. The lights on her visor disappeared. She turned around to say something to Tara and Stacy. CREAAK! The robot moved and Lily nearly lost her balance. She saw that Tara and Stacy had secured themselves into chairs. "If you want to get out, turn around and punch the wall in front of you," Tara said. "This is going to be good," Stacy said. Lily turned around and made a punching motion with her hands. CRACK! The rock wall crumbled into dust and sunlight rushed in. In the distance, Lily could see a building surrounded by dwarves. "Commence run!" she said. Sally surged forward at an amazing speed, leaving the rock chamber far behind. "Let's do this!" Stacy said.

In two minutes the robot reached the building. "Commence manual walk," Lily said. Hologram images of boots appeared over Lily's shoes. She stepped forward and flattened a large group of dwarves. She turned right and ordered the weapons list to show up. Her visor lit up with a list of different weapons. Her eyes locked on a weapon. "Sword!" She called. Lily watched as one of Sally's hands retracted into the wrist, replaced by a wicked-looking sword.

Ping! Ping! The dwarves had begun to fire their weapons. Bullets of light harmlessly bounced off Sally's armor. But Lily wasn't going to take any chances. She deflected the rest of the bullets with her sword and was just about to punch the dwarf building into pieces when the whole thing exploded.

KABOOM! Sally was thrown backward. From the ruins of the dwarf building, another robot emerged. It was the same size as Sally. Tara gasped. "*Carl?*"

Lily climbed to her feet. Carl the robot rushed towards her. At the last second before impact, Lily could see a grim-faced dwarf looking at her through his visor. Lily held up her fist.

BONG! Carl staggered backward and Lily took her chance, jumping on top of Carl and hitting him with her sword. Unfortunately, the sword clanged off Carl's armor, not even scratching. Carl took out a sword of his own, but instead of hitting the armored torso and limbs, he drove the weapon into Sally's left knee.

The effect was immediate. Sally fell onto her side with a groan of metal. Lily's helmet visor glowed red as she tried to get the robot to stand up. As Sally climbed to her feet, Carl charged her again, sword raised. Lily rapidly scrolled through her list of weapons and selected a giant cannon.

The cannon slid out of Sally's other wrist. As it warmed up the sides glowed a bright orange. Momentarily confused, the pilot dwarf brought Carl to a stop. The cannon fired.

KABOOMCREAAK! Super-heated plasma shot out of the cannon. The plasma slammed into Carl, and he toppled over with a sound of creaking and bending metal. When the robot got up again, Lily could see that all of Carl's joints had melted together. Lily swung her sword at the partially disabled robot. The metal blade sank deep through the robot's softened armor, and it went still. The pilot dwarf climbed out of Carl and shook his fists at Lily. She waved back and fell over as Sally was suddenly lifted into the air.

Lily yanked off her helmet as she climbed to her feet. Tara and Stacy had unbuckled their seatbelts. Through Sally's front window, a large spaceship had positioned itself in front of the robot. Ropes were attached to Sally's hands. Lily realized the spaceship was lifting Sally into the air.

Chapter 17: The NPSbot (Nitrogen Powered Super-speed bot)

"We need to get out of here!" Stacy yelled. Tara herded Lily and Stacy down two sets of stairs and yanked open a trapdoor in the floor. The door opened to reveal an escape pod, made for two people. "You two go," Lily said to Tara and Stacy. Before they could protest, Lily ran back up the stairs.

The interior of the cockpit was freezing. Lily realized that Sally was so high up in the sky, the temperature had dropped. A loud hiss told Lily that the escape pod was ejecting. If she didn't go now, she wouldn't get off the robot. Lily sprinted down the stairs and dropped through the trapdoor. The escape pod was already twenty feet away. She tossed the bag of itch grenades into the sky. She wouldn't need them. Lily reached into her pocket and brought out an ultra-explosive grenade she had kept from the war. She pushed it into a bunch of wires running down the wall. The escape pod was now fifty feet away. Pressing the detonation button on the bomb Lily jumped out of the robot as it exploded in a giant ball of fire and debris.

KABOOM! The shockwave from the blast threw Lily towards the escape pod. She slammed into the pod and hung on for dear life as it zoomed away.

Lily tried not to look down as the escape pod passed through several clouds. *Thunk*. Lily glanced to her right and saw a bomb attached to the pod. That was *not* good. She managed to crawl her way over the top of the escape pod. She hung upside-down from the windshield and banged on it. "There's a bomb on the pod!" she screamed. Unfortunately, the wind snatched away most of Lily's words, so her yell sounded more like: "THERE'S ... BOMB ... POD!" A wide-eyed Tara nodded and grabbed two backpacks. She handed one to Stacy and pulled a lever. A hatch popped open on the top of the pod and Tara and Stacy shot out of it. Lily jumped and grabbed Tara's foot. A parachute sprouted out of Stacy's backpack. Tara activated her own parachute. Their free-fall slowed down to a controlled descent. Above them, the grenade exploded. Surprisingly, there was no fire but magma. In fifteen seconds the escape pod was a blob of melted metal, which plummeted down to the ground one hundred feet below. As Lily and Tara watched the fiery wreck tumble down to earth, Stacy cleared her throat. "Well," she said, "do you have any idea when we will get to the ground?" The problem was, they didn't.

Chapter 18

Fid the fortune teller

Jake was *not* having a good day.

Even in the sweltering heat, the dwarves fought on. Most of the elves had collapsed from heat exhaustion, and the elves still fighting didn't seem to be any better. Of course, there was the real problem: the elves' control center manager and an officer who happened to be one of Jake's best comrades had gone missing. To make things worse, Lily, the human girl the elves took from earth, had vanished with them.

The dwarves stampeded the elves, kicking up dust. Jake blindly fired his dart gun until a dwarf ran right into him, and he fell over with a yell of surprise.

When Jake finally managed to get up again (darn, those dwarves were *too* good at trampling people), the dwarves were not too far away, clambering over the ruins of the city wall and whooping and yelling like monkeys. Elves chased after them, but Jake knew one hundred elves weren't going to do much against an army of one thousand dwarves. He brushed the dust off his clothes and ran after the dwarves.

Ten minutes later, the dwarves had reached the central tower. As they charged straight through the door, Jake veered off course and headed into a nearby tiny house. He yanked open the door and pushed his way past various glass jars on shelves (which promptly fell and broke) and a big metal sign that read: *THE FUTURE IS YOUR DESTINY!* (Which toppled over and nearly whacked him on the head).

Jake reached an empty counter topped with a big glass sphere. He knocked on the counter and an elf popped up from behind it. The elf had wrinkly ears and a long nose. "Hello!" The tiny elf had a creaky voice that sounded like a mouse farting, only louder and squeakier. "Fid DeFazio," Jake said. "I have a question for you." "Is your question about the future?" Fid asked. "No!" "Fortune charms?" "Are you kidding me?!?"

Fid glared at Jake. "I'm just a fortune teller. I can only help you with things about fortune and the fut-"

"Don't you dare lie to me," Jake growled. "You may be a fortune teller, but I know that you are also a gadget collector." Fid snorted. "What's with all the funny talk, Jake Iander? I'm just what I say." "Shut up, DeFazio."

***

When Lily, Tara, and Stacy touched down in the grass, the sun was setting. Lily extracted herself from the tangled parachute and got to her feet. "Where *are* we?" she asked.

Good question. The landscape that stretched out in front of them was nearly barren, except for a few dried up shrubs. Far away on the horizon, there was a thin line of buildings, indicating that there was life somewhere in this bleak place. "Fifty bucks and a year's worth of candy that's the dwarf city," Stacy said. "Of course not," Tara chided. "That line in the distance is obviously the elfin city." The two argued about taking bets and just how important candy was while Lily kicked dead shrubs into dust. As the argument intensified, Lily began to get bored. She put on her bossiest, I'm-in-charge-so-you-better-listen-to-me voice and said, "That is *enough*. You two stop arguing right this instant!"

The effect was immediate and satisfying. Tara and Stacy stopped talking and glared at each other, but the argument was over. "We *have* to find out what that line in the distance is," Lily said. With a reluctant sigh they started over the bare ground.

Chapter 19

The secret entrance

Lily staggered across the ground, her eyelids half closed. How long had they been walking? Next to her, Tara and Stacy trekked across the rock-hard dirt. The dark line in the distance didn't seem to be getting any closer. In fact, it seemed to be moving *away* from them. Lily kicked at a bush hard in frustration. She expected it to turn into dust, but instead her foot connected with a metal clang. She hopped away, cussing as she grabbed her sore foot. Stacy and Tara leaned over the bush with interest. Stacy nudged the metal shrub. It didn't budge. A thoughtful look came onto her face. "I remember reading something about a metal shrub in a dried-up place ... ," she said. She leaned over and started to count the leaves. "Oh, get out of the way," Tara said. Her eyes flickered over the metal leaves. She grabbed a single leaf and pulled it out of the bush.

CREEAKK! Everybody covered their ears as the bush crumbled into a pile of dust, rust, and nails. The debris spilled into a hidden shaft and disappeared. Tara ran forward and inspected the hole. There was enough wriggle room for all three of them to go down in single file. "When did that hole get there?" Lily asked. "I don't know," Stacy said. Her tone began to get more excited. "Perhaps this hole was built in the ancient times, when Yedwab the elf ruled the city. They must have made a secret entrance, a tunnel, by placing a plate over the hole and a metal bush on top of the plate. When Tara pulled out the leaf the bush crumbled, but the plate disintegrated along with it. But why would they build a hidden tunnel in a place like *this*?" Stacy waved her hands expansively at the landscape around her.

Lily, who hadn't been paying attention much, nodded like she had understood whatever Stacy had just said. She asked, "Who wants to go down first?" The three had a silent but fierce staring contest and when Stacy won, Lily had another contest with Tara. Unfortunately for Tara, Lily won. "Oh, all right, I'll go," Tara snapped. She pressed her arms to her sides and jumped through the hole.

Tara slid through the hole and kept going down at a fast pace like friction didn't exist. Before Lily could yell a warning, Tara had disappeared into the depths of the dirt tunnel. "We have to see where the tunnel leads," she said. Lily suddenly had a fear of being left behind. "I'll go next," she said. She pressed her arms against her body and jumped into the hole.

Tips for jumping down an unknown tunnel: don't. The dirt shaft stretched on forever. There wasn't enough space for Lily to move her arms, so she was getting quite cramped. She zoomed down the dark tunnel. Just when she thought that the shaft would never end, it did. Lily shot out of the tunnel opening and landed face-first in a pile of dirt. She climbed to her feet and spat out a mouthful of dirt. Nearby, Tara scowled. "Where *were* you?" she asked. "I've been waiting for *ages*."

Lily opened her mouth to reply, and an inhumane scream pierced her ears. She clapped her hands over the sides of her face as the noise got louder and shriller. Tara stared at the tunnel opening. With a very loud shriek, Stacy flew out of the hole that was the tunnel opening. For two seconds she froze, suspended in mid-air. Then gravity took hold of her, and Stacy crashed to the ground, flattening Lily. "Ow," Lily muttered. Stacy rolled off her and stood up. "Well," she said, "now that we're down here, what do we do now?"

Chapter 20

The eon-old dirt

Tara, Stacy, and Lily walked past the piles of dust down a small corridor made of dirt. Lily kept looking up at the ceiling, afraid it would collapse on top of them. Ten minutes later, the tunnel opened up into a cavernous chamber filled with more dust. "I don't understand," Stacy said. "There should be something down here. I think it was an eon-old map to get back outside." "There's some eon-old dirt in here," Lily offered.

Tara kicked the nearest dirt pile, and it exploded in a cloud of dust. "We're never going to get out of here," she said. "Hey, guys, what's that?" Lily had spotted the thin outline of a rectangle, made of light. They crossed over to it. "I think that's our exit," Stacy said. "Right," Tara said. "Stand back." She backed up, ran at the wall and did a high kick while jumping up into the air. A section of dirt crumbled and daylight streamed through the gap. Unfortunately, the rest of the chamber started to disintegrate, too.

Chunks of dirt began to fall from the dirt ceiling, smashing into piles of dust. A big piece of dirt fell and crashed into the largest of the dirt piles. POOF! A massive cloud of dust flew up and settled all over the chamber. Coughing, Stacy desperately began to widen the hole in the wall, breaking off chunks of dirt with her hands. With the help of Lily and Tara, the hole was soon wide enough for them to go through. Lily clambered through the gap, closely followed by Tara and Stacy.

Chapter 20: The eon old dirt

They got out not a moment too soon. One second after Stacy's foot had left the chamber the room collapsed, sending a giant wave of dust through the air. When the dirt stampede finally ended, Lily was covered head to toe in a layer of dust. It would take a million years to get all that dirt off her face. She opened her mouth to speak and swallowed a gallon of dust. Lily spat on the ground and groaned.

***

Fid DeFazio led Jake to a door hidden behind a wall made of assorted glass containers. The tiny elf kicked a bottom jar, and the whole wall fell over. Amazingly, none of the jars shattered. "Plastic wall," Fid explained. He pulled open the door.

The door led to a world of dangerous collectables. Tables and tables were piled with weapons, hopefully deactivated bombs and many other deadly gadgets. Jake happened to glance to his right and saw a familiar-looking sword. He picked it up from the table it rested on. "My sword," he said. "You had it all these years." He still remembered the day he dropped it in a piranha-infested lake after tripping over a rock. And now, twenty years later, here it was. "Yep," Fid said. Jake pointed his sword at him. "Did you steal all these weapons from elfin warriors?" he asked. "Nope," Fid answered, but afterwards he fidgeted around whenever Jake glanced at a peculiar weapon.

Jake grabbed a sheath from yet another table. "Are we there yet?" he asked. "I don't know," Fid said, his raspy voice dripping with sarcasm. "In fact, I have absolutely no idea why you came he - Ow!" Jake kicked Fid in the butt with his foot. "You know perfectly well why I came here," he said. As Fid hopped around and whined like a sad puppy, Jake suddenly saw an old, beaten-up wooden box lying on the floor. Before Fid could yell *what are you doing* he snatched up the container and pried it open. Carefully enclosed in dark gray velvet was one long pill.

"The pill of poison," he said. Jake turned to Fid. "Millennia ago one of the ancient elfin leaders ordered a dwarf to create a pill for everlasting magic. The chosen dwarf made the pill, but the builder gave it a completely different purpose: when inserted into a special slot in a dwarf vault a specialized gas would spread across the world, wiping out all elves." He turned the box upside-down, and the pill clattered to the floor. Jake picked it up and tossed it into the nearest trash can. "But the elf leader didn't trust the dwarf anyway, so he had it destroyed and put a plastic pill in the box." He left without any further conversation.

As soon as Jake had exited Fid's shed of a house, he slammed the door, which was a mistake. Several dwarves appeared across from the building, alerted by the loud noise. Jake ran towards the forest, ducking under trees and swerving towards where he thought the battlefield was. Five minutes later, he came out of the forest, looked in front of him, and groaned in frustration. He had somehow managed to run in the exact opposite direction of the battlefield. He could tell, because there was smoke and the roar of fighting rising above the gray undergrowth and trees. Jake was standing on a hill. Below him stretched a very unimpressive barren landscape. Dried-up bushes lay on the rock-hard dirt. A rustling sound startled him. He turned. A tree branch had broken off, and it lay on the ground. Jake turned his back to the forest and faced the barren landscape to take a rest. Little did he know he was about to have one of the biggest surprises of his life.

Chapter 21

The biggest surprise

Lily, Tara, and Stacy walked across the dry ground. Ever since the dirt cavern imploded, there had been quite a bit of trouble getting the dust out of their hair and clothes. The sun beat down hotter than ever, and the dirt on their skin provided an atmosphere that kept the heat in. Lily wiped mud and sweat off her forehead. "This place should be named the land of everlasting dry dirt," she complained. Stacy nodded as Tara smacked a lazy mosquito away from her face.

She looked up. "What is that?" Tara pointed to a gray hill in front of a forest not too far away. A figure sat on the top. As they watched two short people (probably dwarves) seized his arms. The figure yelped in shock, and Lily spotted a dark blue cape. "Jake," Tara said. "Only he could wear that ridiculous cape," Lily agreed. Stacy knitted her brows in concentration as an unconscious Jake disappeared into the forest along with the two dwarves. "We should follow them," she said. They ran for the hill.

***

Jake was taken by surprise. The dwarves seemed to appear out of nowhere, simply leaping out of the trees and grabbing his arms. As Jake yelled, "Hey!" the biggest of the dwarves knocked him out with a fist.

Jake opened his eyes. At least a million pairs of eyes looked right back at him. Dwarf eyes. He jumped to his feet and unsheathed his sword. He was in a packed room. The crowd of dwarves suddenly omitted a roar of battle and charged him. Jake would be fighting one against a million. *This is a stupid way to fight*, he thought. He raised his sword and, feeling quite silly, jumped into the chaos.

He hacked his way through the dwarves, occasionally booting an unsuspecting dwarf in his rear end. He was starting to get the hang of it when another wave of yells flooded into the room. Another thousand dwarves appeared, and this time they clutched weapons in their hairy fists. That couldn't be good. Jake kicked a weapon out of a dwarf's hand and took hold of his wrist, throwing him into his tiny comrades. He was now fighting with two blades instead of one. Luckily, the dwarves liked to jump, or Jake would have had to lean down to hit them. It seemed only minutes before arms began to get tired. The sound of ripping cloth startled him. He turned around to find that his blue cloak was now riddled with holes. Stupid dwarves.

***

Tara clambered up the hill, Lily and Stacy following close behind. She leaped over tree roots and rocks. Once she tripped and almost smashed her face into a tree. But they kept running. Up ahead she could see the elfin city. They were almost there. Then things went terribly wrong. Suddenly there was no grass under Tara's feet. She fell into a hole. Stacy and Lily joined her with a lot of screaming, too shocked to stop themselves. "*Shush!*" Tara hissed. She scanned their surroundings. They seemed to be in a large chamber constructed of stone. There was a great yelling sound that looked as though it came from everywhere. Then Tara's eyes got adjusted to the darkness. The yells came from dwarves. Thousands of them. They were packed together in the large room. Most were empty handed, but a few had weapons. Tara, Stacy, and Lily were standing on a hidden platform in the chamber's corner. But what were they fighting? As Tara looked into the massive crowd, Stacy screamed, "Look!"

Tara followed Stacy's finger and saw Jake, wielding two sword. Lily frowned. "How can Jake hold back *that* many dwarves?" Tara knew she was right. Jake's cloak was in tatters. He also had a bunch of cuts and scratches on his face. Tara was positive he couldn't fight any longer. "Arm yourselves," she said. Stacy and Lily patted their empty pockets. They must have lost their weapons during the collapsing dirt chamber. Even Tara had lost her plentiful supply of grenades. She unleashed a round of creative cussing and turned to the others. "We'll go in fighting." Stacy looked shocked. "With no weapons?" "We could get weapons from dwarves," Lily said. "Let's stick with that," Tara concluded. They jumped off the platform. "Yeah," Lily muttered. "We're just awesome at kicking dwarf butt."

***

Lily wanted to run into a little dark corner and hide.

Of *course*, she wanted to help her friends, but against this many dwarves? That was a bit over the top. Lily punched and kicked dwarves while Tara danced around like a gymnast, throwing dwarves. As for Stacy, she ran around, tripping dwarves and kicking them as they tried to stand up. Once or twice, Lily would have to dive wildly out of the way to avoid being trampled. A current of air whooshed through the chamber, ruffling her hair. Wait ... where did the wind come from? The air seemed to blow from the opposite direction of the big hole above. Then Lily saw it. A small tunnel, the size of a car door, was on the far side of the chamber. A faint stream of daylight was visible through it.

Our exit, Lily thought. A *clang* of metal rang behind her and she spun on her heel. "Jake!" she yelled. Unfortunately, the yell scared Jake more than it alerted him. He turned around and nearly whacked her with his sword. "Hey!" Lily protested. "Do I *sound* like a dwarf?"

***

Stacy didn't know how to fight.

She obviously could punch and kick, but that was general stuff. *Everybody* could do that. She wasn't like Tara. Tara could jump into the air and smash two dwarf heads together while booting two more dwarf butts. Stacy could barely manage to block a swing from a weapon. Then she heard Lily's voice: "Do I *sound* like a dwarf?" "Sorry!" Jake yelled. Stacy stifled a laugh. Lily as a dwarf? Hilarious.

"Stacy!" Tara shouted. Stacy turned around. Tara pushed her way through the massive dwarf army, with Jake and Lily following close behind. "Lily says she found an exit," Jake yelled. Lily screamed as a dwarf almost hit her with a spiked club. Tara pointed to her left at a small tunnel with daylight streaming through. "I have a way to get there," she said. "So how *do* we get there?" Stacy said. She wished she hadn't asked. Tara gave her one of those evil smiles that made her think: *Are you the villain?* Then she stepped on a dwarf's head and began running over the dwarf heads, leaping over gaps in the crowd. Jake and Stacy groaned while Lily loudly complained: "Is Tara mad? Why can't there be an easier way?" But eventually, they agreed to follow Tara's example.

At first, the dwarves went silent as they ran over their heads. Then the yells of protest and terror began to rise.

"Ow!"

"My poor head!"

"Mommy!"

Finally, Stacy reached the tunnel, where Tara was waiting. "Took you long enough," she grumped. *Whatever*, Stacy thought. They squeezed through the tunnel. Once or twice Stacy would hit her head on the tunnel top and feel sympathy for the dwarves. But still: they *had* stepped on those dwarves for a good reason, right?

Chapter 22

The totally embarrassing attack

Jake hit his head at least fifty times on the tunnel before they finally tumbled out of the crawl space in a heap. As his annoying older brother Parker would say: *Dude, how can you manage to hit your head fifty times in a row without getting knocked out? I mean, seriously?* Maybe for once, Parker did have a point.

Stacy, Tara, and Lily slowly got up from their human pile. Five seconds later, they were talking to Jake like *very* angry mothers. "Jake Iander, what in the *world* were you thinking?" Tara demanded. "Going against all those dwarves all by yourself ... I'd rather go with a group of people myself," Stacy said. "You are much too young to be picking fights," Lily declared. "Whatever," Jake muttered. "*What* did you say?" all three girls said at once. As he opened his mouth to say something an evil cackle startled him.

"Ha!" A dwarf stood no more than ten feet away, wielding a brass club with a worn leather grip and steel spikes. The surprised but now alert group rose unsteadily. Stacy hid a dwarf's knife she had stolen behind her back. Lily enclosed a pile of dirt in her hand. Tara reviewed her numerous headlocks and throws, and Jake slowly drew his sword. The dwarf laughed. "You think you can defeat me, the leader of the dwarves? This is too funny. Let's play a little game. I'll give you two hours to hide in the maze, and then I'll come looking for you." "You despicable dwarves," Jake snarled. "I'll-" "What maze?" Stacy asked. The dwarf smiled and threw his club.

The club smashed a withered bush into dust and screws rolled everywhere. A metal bush was *not* a good sign. In ten seconds the ground underneath them had caved in and they fell through, landing on a stone floor. Lily groaned and sat up. The dwarf had disappeared. Around them, walls stretched out. The walls seemed to form a rock labyrinth, complete with dead ends and potholes. Tara swore. "We're supposed to play hide and seek in *that*?" I guess so," Stacy replied. A war horn blew and the game began.

As soon as the horn sounded, Tara yelled, "Split up!" As they took a step forward, the walls around them shifted, so now there was only one corridor with numerous stone trenches. "Never mind," Tara muttered as Lily started through the tunnel.

If you think Lily was brave, you're wrong. Lily started running because she had felt that they would be in big danger if they stayed there. Before long, Jake, Stacy, and Tara had caught up with her. The corridor began to widen as they sprinted over the stone ground. Five minutes in, a trip wire sent Lily sprawling. "Duck, people!" Jake yelled as whistling sounds filled the air. Stacy pushed Lily into a trench as Tara tripped and crashed into Jake, who fell into another trench as arrows filled the air, sinking into the stone walls with a dull *thunk*. Lily crouched as cage doors topped with sharp metal points slid over the trenches. They were trapped.

Chapter 23

An awesome escape

The smell of food made Lily open her eyes. She must've fallen asleep from boredom. A small pear lay in the trench. Apparently, Stacy had already eaten because she was wide awake, finishing off the last of a pear. "I don't think it's poisoned," Stacy said. "Yum!" Lily wolfed down her snack in a second. The cage doors were still fastened tight over their trench, and Stacy said that they wouldn't budge. Lily finished the pear and the door above suddenly slid open.

"Out!" Lily hissed. Stacy clambered out of the hole as Tara and Jake appeared at the edge of the trench. "We should go," Jake noticed as the bottom of the trench caved in just as Lily climbed out. "Yeah." Lily agreed with a shudder. They jogged through the maze, which had morphed into a labyrinth again. They started down a random hall as unknown gas blocked the area behind them. They turned a corner and the maze instantly disappeared, leaving Lily standing in a patch of sunlight.

"What the-" Lily blinked the spots out of her eyes. The dwarf stood in front of them. For some reason, he had a look of disappointment on his face. "I've been watching you for just about forever," he complained. "I want to have some fun!" "I'll give you some fun, you little-" Jake growled. "Language!" Stacy interrupted. "Whatever." The dwarf hefted his club. Jake stepped forward and a flash of silver cut the dwarf's club in half. Jake sheathed his sword. The dwarf just laughed and spread his arms. Instantly, small black figures, probably dwarves, surrounded them. They looked strangely familiar. Lily thought it was kind of stupid of them to not bring weapons. A horrible thought struck her. "Man, the Fighters were dwarves? That just sucks," she complained. The leader dwarf grinned evilly. "Have you ever thought why there have been no Fighter invasions in the past seven hours?" Jake gripped his sword so tightly, his knuckles whitened. "Are we going to fight them or not?" he said. "We are," Tara said. They charged the dwarves.

Two seconds later ...

The fight was full of violence, but Lily and her friends didn't get hurt. Every once in a while Jake, Lily, Stacy, and Tara would scream stuff like, "AHHHHH! OH YEAH! EAT THE DUST, SUCKERS! AHHHHHH!" Most dwarves stood frozen in shock and fear until Jake's sword hit their little dwarf butts or Stacy punched their faces. They would wail afterwards, waddling away and screaming for their mommies. Once or twice dwarves got past Tara's defenses and bruised her leg with a kick but she would recover quickly and teach the tiny troublemakers a lesson. The leader dwarf had stepped back to watch the show, but his smile was fading, replaced by a fierce but nervous scowl. Tara ducked to avoid a jumping dwarf (which meant almost flattening your face against the ground because the dwarves jumped so low) and made her way to the dwarf.

When Tara reached the dwarf, she instantly captured him in a complicated headlock. In about five seconds she had neatly thrown the dwarf backward to the ground so hard dust flew. Then Lily punched him and he blacked out. Tara turned around to admire their work. All the dwarves who had dared battle them were knocked out and snoring.

Jake whistled. "*That* is a whole new record of butt-kicking." They walked toward the elfin city in the distance.

Chapter 24

Why Lily was taken from Earth

Halfway to the elfin city, Tara and Jake started whispering to each other.

Lily could only catch a few words, like "war" and "freaking dwarves". Then she heard Jake mutter, "I really do think that we shouldn't have dragged Lily into this war. We did only take her from Earth for a simple reason."

Lily looked up. "What are you talking about?" "Uh ... you probably might not remember this, but there was this night where you were looking out of a window a few years back ..." Tara said. Lily searched her memory and remembered she was looking out of her bedroom when she was about twelve. Two people had climbed out of a hole the sidewalk and were looking around. One, a woman, had seen her and said something to the other person. He glanced at Lily and they both jumped back into the hole and disappeared.

Lily snapped out of her flashback. "Those people on the sidewalk that other night ... that was you?" Jake and Tara both nodded. "So you took me from Earth because I saw an elf?" More nods. "Only because I trust you, I'm not going ask any more questions," Lily concluded. But she couldn't help thinking, *what an inconvenient truth*. She ran for the elfin city, ready for anything. Which was good, because she would need her bravery.

As soon as they stepped over what was left of the northern tower wall, an alarm sounded from nowhere. Ten armed dwarves ran forward and handcuffed Tara and Jake. "Off to the dungeons!" one dwarf said cheerfully. "We never built a dungeon!" Jake complained. No one noticed that Lily and Stacy had disappeared.

"Let's go!" Lily hissed. She and Stacy sprinted to the hole where the eastern tower door once was and clambered through. Stacy scowled when she saw all the rubble. "Stupid dwarves," she muttered. As they ran through a hallway voices sounded right in front of them.

Stacy pulled Lily behind a door as the dwarves led Tara and Jake down the hallway. They were both tied up, but Jake had somehow managed to grab his sword. As they walked he accidentally tripped and dropped his sword. The blade clanged on the floor. A dwarf smirked. When their backs were turned Lily did a very daring thing: she rolled out of the doorway and snatched up the sword. When she had rolled back to safety, she angled the sword so it reflected the hallway light, shining on Jake's face. He blinked and glanced ever so slightly to his right. When he saw Stacy waving and Lily holding his sword, he made a face and mouthed *help us get out of here now* before turning back to the dwarves.

Suddenly Lily realized that they would have to free Jake and Tara before they reached the dungeons, wherever that was. "We need to make a distraction," she whispered to Stacy. Stacy shook her head. "I have to get to the control center," she replied. Lily took one last look at the dwarves and followed Stacy down the hallway.

Luckily, the control center was empty for the moment, but Lily knew it wouldn't be long until a dwarf came through the doorway. They went over to the room where they had made the skin rash grenades. Stacy crossed over to a table where a bunch of metal scraps and wire lay. She gathered up an armful of the stuff and carried them over to another table in a corner. She turned to Lily. "If this works right, you won't get electrocuted." Stacy began to work, attaching wires and using a solder gun to meld pieces of metal.

Ten minutes later, she held up a metal rod. Lily could see that there were no wires sticking out. "Am I supposed to whack dwarves with this?" she asked. Stacy gave her the elfin stink-eye and returned to her work. She grabbed a thin tube filled with clear liquid and inserted it into one end of the metal stick. Opening a compartment on the bottom, she pulled out two tiny metal sticks. Stacy colored one stick red and another stick yellow with some markers. She frowned. "I'm sorry, Lily, but it will take too long to explain how to use this device. You can have this." Stacy handed Lily a loudspeaker.

Lily stared at the loudspeaker. "That's it?" "Yes," Stacy replied, "but be careful. That loudspeaker is *very* loud. It's in the name." After some protests from Lily, they finally ran out of the door and to the dungeons ... if there actually was a dungeon.

Two minutes later, Lily spotted Tara's boot heel disappearing behind a doorway. She peered around the corner. The dwarves stood in a gray cell with dust and no windows. One dwarf held a key, and Lily was pretty sure it wasn't for Jake and Tara's handcuffs. *Here goes*, she thought. She stepped back and yelled, "YO!" into the loudspeaker.

The sound that came out was enough to make Stacy clap her hands over her ears and for Jake to fall over on his face. Tara also fell over. The dwarves screamed and danced around in the cell, their hands over their ears. Lily screamed into the loudspeaker: "*SURRENDER! THERE IS NO ESCAPE FROM MY AWESOMENESS. DROP YOUR WEAPONS AND GIVE ME ALL YOUR MONEY.*"

The words worked like magic. The dwarves had no money, but they dropped their weapons. The key to the cell was buried under a pile of dust (the gray fuzzy kind in an old basement, not dirt). The terrified dwarves backed against the wall. Lily used her sword - sorry, *Jake's* sword - to cut through Jake and Tara's handcuffs. Jake, dazed from shock, mumbled something like "I have no money," as Tara helped him to his feet. Stacy grinned and Lily tried her best not to crack up. About five seconds later, her shoe unearthed the cell key. After they all had gone out through the door, Lily smiled at the dwarves. "Enjoy prison," she said and locked the cell door. Stacy melted the lock with her flamethrower gun before sending a massive electric charge into the room.

Chapter 25

The collapsing tower

Jake wanted to kick himself.

First of all, Tara just *had* to trip and send him painfully into a trench - that was no accident. Second, he should've remembered to keep his sword out *before* he got handcuffed. At least he could have *some* kind of defense against the dwarves. But wait! There was more! Lily had "borrowed" his sword and ran away with Stacy to save him and Tara. The nerve that he needed to be rescued by girls ... ugh! Jake had gotten his sword back, though Lily didn't look too happy about it.

"Don't expect me to steal your sword again. It's not like I'm going to bust out some moves every time I have to rescue you," Lily told him. "I don't need rescuing," Jake protested. "Oh, yes, you do. You're just a little baby, remember?" Lily smiled. This led to some very creative swearing in Elfin from Jake. Stacy covered her ears and Tara groaned. When he finally stopped elf cussing, he said, "I hope you did not understand that." Lily winced. "Don't worry. I got the gist."

Meanwhile, Stacy peeked out of a window. "Well, the good news is, the elves probably haven't gone extinct, and the candy store is still open," she reported. "What the crap?" Lily muttered. Stacy continued: "The bad news is, dwarves are everywhere, and there seems to be nothing that can stop them." "Oh, dang it!" Tara barked.

Suddenly, a girl about Lily's age with long blonde hair stumbled around the corner. She was definitely an elf. Seconds later a man with spiky brown hair and a long nose followed. Jake stepped forward. "What news of the elves?" he asked. The long-nosed dude answered, "Most are wounded, but there are still some fighters out behind the towers." "But there are still many dwarves in the city," the blonde girl added. Jake sighed. "Better than I thought. Well, then-"

BANG! The tower began to crumble, the ceiling caving in and the walls creaking. "Ann, Will, run!" Tara yelled. The blonde girl and the long-nosed dude darted down the corridor. A section of ceiling above Jake cracked, threatening to collapse. Lily pulled Jake's sword right out of his sheath - so much for keeping promises - and chucked it at a large piece of stone as it fell. The blade intercepted the rock, breaking it into smaller pieces so they bounced harmlessly off Jake's head. Then something hard smacked into his forehead and he blacked out.

Tara yanked Stacy to one side as rubble smashed through the floor. Lily screamed as a rock hit Jake's head with a *thunk*. He fell to the floor unconscious. Lily picked up his sword from the floor. Stacy scrambled away from a hole in the ground. "We can't stay here any longer!" she yelled. Tara high-kicked a rock into dust and dragged Jake next to Stacy. The floor suddenly tilted at a nauseating angle, throwing Tara out of a broken window. Lily pressed herself against the wall along with Stacy and Jake, but Tara was hanging on to the windowsill with two fingers. Then the tower tilted to the right and Lily tumbled out of the window, dislodging Tara from her ledge as she fell past.

Chapter 26

The endless fall

One hundred fifty stories into the clouds.

That's how tall the eastern tower was. Tara wondered what her chances of surviving the fall were. Next to her, Lily screamed and twisted in mid-air, barely dodging a piece of falling rubble. Her hair whipped around her face. Somehow, she had managed to keep hold of Jake's sword and the loudspeaker. In front of Tara's eyes, the tower fell apart. Metal and rocks flew everywhere. She saw Stacy roll a still-knocked-out Jake to the cracked bridge connecting the towers to the central tower. Stacy managed to drag Jake across the bridge and into the central tower just as the bridge crumbled into pieces.

Truth be told, Tara wasn't surprised that the tower had collapsed. The weak wooden foundations underneath the building had rotted almost to nonexistence years ago. She just hadn't anticipated it would happen so soon. The wind screamed louder than Lily, stinging her face and numbing her fingers. Below them, the elfin city stretched - a crowded landscape of houses and elves. Right now elves were probably screaming and running around in circles or gawking up at the rain of rubble. The tower just *had* to fall in the direction of an inhabited area.

A flash of silver caught Tara's eye and she fell onto something hard with a loud *thump*. She had fallen on top of a giant spaceship with Lily next to her. A compartment opened and Tara dropped through. Stacy sat in the aircraft's cockpit. When she looked at Tara and Lily, the color rushed back into her pale face. "Oh, I'm so glad you're here! I thought I would be too slow and-" "Be glad you weren't," Tara said. "How do you feel?" Stacy asked. "Better than me, probably," a voice said.

Jake emerged from the back of the aircraft. A red bump had risen up on his forehead where the rock had hit him. He had gotten rid of his cape, which either meant he didn't want it anymore or it was too damaged and it fell off by itself. "How do *you* feel?" Lily said. Jake gingerly touched the bump on his head and winced. "There's a splitting headache going on in my head." "Uh ... do you want your sword back?" Lily asked. Jake shook his head. "You can keep it. Just give it back after this war ends." He unbuckled his sheath and tossed it to Lily. Unfortunately, Jake's head injury had screwed up his aim and Lily wasn't paying attention so the sheath smacked her in the face. "Ow!" she complained. As she fastened it around her waist, Stacy said, "Guys, we have to concentrate! Any minute now the tower rubble will crush the town. We need a plan!"

Tara ran to the window and swore. Stacy was right. Chunks of debris had already smashed into the ground, narrowly missing innocent elves. Lily ran over to the window and opened it, yelling into her loudspeaker: "*ELVES! IF YOU DON'T WANT TO BE CRUSHED BY ABOUT A MILLION TONS OF RUBBLE, RUN!*" The words tore through the wind like tissue paper and the elves below panicked, evacuating the city as fast as they could. Thankfully, no one questioned why there was a giant spaceship hovering above them.

Tara stepped back and hit her head on the wall (which hurt) then stubbed her toe on the floor (which also hurt). As she cussed and stumbled around, Stacy dived towards the falling tower debris, professionally maneuvering through the rocks and metal that tumbled through the air. Tara clutched her stomach, trying not to throw up as the aircraft did an unexpected turn. Lily staggered backward and dropped her loudspeaker. Her pale face was starting to turn green. "I *hate* flying!" she yelled. "Well, too bad," Stacy said as she gripped the controls, her eyes staring straight out of the front windshield. Tara suddenly lost her balance and fell over. Jake slid across the floor. "What's going on?" he shouted. "I don't know!" Tara shouted back.

That was when the aircraft started to roll in the air.

Chapter 27

Stacy takes her aircraft for a *very* dangerous joyride

Stacy flew her aircraft through the falling rocks, clutching the piloting levers. A giant rock appeared in front of her windshield and she yelled, "Crap!" before pulling the controls to the right. The spaceship made a sharp turn and continued on its way. Stacy's plan was to somehow get to the northern tower, where most of the elves would have gathered and where she could get help. Sometimes a rock would crack the windshield and Stacy would have to yank the reverse lever backward before it could punch a hole in the glass. She floored the gas and dodged a giant rock. In front of her, there was a gap in the rocks, just big enough for the spaceship to get through. If she was fast enough, she could get into the region of the more spaced out rocks. Stacy gritted her teeth, flipped open a button cover, checked her seatbelt, and pressed the button, which was labeled **roll**.

***

Jake slid across the floor and yelled to Tara, "What's going on?" "I don't know!" Tara replied. *Well, that's just great*, he thought. He was wondering why in the *world* Stacy was driving through the falling tower rubble so fast when the aircraft started to roll wildly. Jake flew into the air and slammed into the ceiling - ouch - and then just as suddenly changed direction and slammed into the wall. Lily yelled, "Ow. Ow.

Ow. Ow! Oh, no - OW!" as she tumbled around in the aircraft. Her loudspeaker flew through the air and nearly whacked Jake in the head. Tara had curled herself into a ball so that she bounced safely off the walls without screaming in pain. Jake grabbed the pilot chair as he flew past the cockpit and yelled, "Stacy! What - ow - are you - ow - doing? Ow!" as he smacked against the back of the chair. Stacy, who - lucky her - was in seatbelts, continued to calmly maneuver the spaceship. Her message couldn't have been clearer: *Go away. I'm working, can't you see?*

The spaceship made another roll. Lily's loudspeaker slammed into Jake. He let go of the chair and slid across the floor. Tara bounced off him as she sailed by, knocking him into Lily, who yelled in surprise and shoved him into a wall. The air filled the word 'ow' as Jake, Lily, and Tara smacked into each other and tumbled off into opposite directions. Then suddenly the rolling stopped as Stacy hit the brakes. Jake crashed into the pilot chair, Lily was hurled into the front windshield, and Tara uncurled herself just as she slammed into the floor and came to rest against the wall, groaning. Stacy grinned. "See?" she said. "That wasn't so bad-" "Oh, *yes* it was!" Lily interrupted. "-anyway, we shall be arriving at the northern tower in approximately ten minutes. Thank you for joining us on the flight of the *Alpha 201*," Stacy continued. "You're very welcome," Jake grumbled.

Tara complained from the floor, "Why did I agree to do this?" "I saved your life, remember?" Stacy said. She glanced out of the front windshield. "Okay, we have arrived at the northern tower," she reported. Stacy landed the *Alpha 201* on the ground and Jake stumbled out through the door, Lily and Tara walking behind him. "I'll stay here, just in case you need a ride," Stacy said. She tossed Lily her loudspeaker. "If you need me, yell," she advised.

Lily caught the loudspeaker and pried open the tower door with her borrowed sword. Immediately, elfin guards blocked her path, swords crossed. Jake stepped forward. "Swords down," he commanded, "we are survivors from the war. We are not going to cause any harm." The elves uncrossed their swords and they ran into the tower.

The tower was packed with elves. A young medic rushed forward. "Oh, Jake, when will you stop hitting your head?" she said crossly when she saw the bump on his head. Another elf grinned. "Your sister's right. I mean, dude, how can you hit your head about a million times in a row without getting knocked out?" "Shut up, Parker," Jake muttered, "I only got knocked out once or twice." Parker grinned.

"Oneida, why don't you take care of your older brother?" Tara suggested. Oneida grinned mischievously and dragged a protesting Jake into the elf crowd. An older elf pushed her way towards them. "Tara!" she said. Parker suddenly looked nervous and said, "I'll be, um, just over there." He ran into the crowd and disappeared. The older elf ran to Tara and gave her a big hug. "Mom!" Tara complained. "Oh, honey, I'm just so glad you're safe!" Tara's mother said. "Oh, go away, mother, you're embarrassing me." Tara grabbed Lily's hand and pulled her into the crowd.

Lily said, "You're mom's, um, really nice." "You can say that again," Tara grumbled. Nearby Oneida was making Jake sit in a chair with an ice pack on his head. "Now, Jake, you can sit down and take some rest," she cooed. "I don't need rest!" Jake said. Spotting Lily and Tara, he begged, "Tara, Lily, help me!" Lily came over and grabbed Jake's younger sister, swinging her into the air. Oneida giggled with delight as Jake jumped out of his chair, tossing his ice pack over his shoulder.

Chapter 27: Stacy takes her aircraft for a *very* dangerous joyride

Lily set Oneida down. "We should go to our living quarters," Jake said. They went over to the service booth, where a small wrinkly elf sat. They waited in line. When it was Jake's turn, he said, "Fid, I could arrest you for many reasons, but right now I need a room." The old elf chuckled. "Alright, Jake, I'll give you room 3765," he said. Lily pushed her way out of the crowd and yelled into her loudspeaker, "*STACY! COME ON DOWN, WE'RE GETTING OUR LIVING QUARTERS ASSIGNED.*"

After Stacy had come out of the aircraft, Fid assigned the girls their rooms. When he saw Lily, he said, "You're Lily, right? I've heard about you. Okay, I'll give you the luxury room 3849." Tara got luxury room 3837 and Stacy got luxury room 3839. As Jake complained why all the girls get the luxury rooms Lily went up a hallway to room 3849 and unlocked the door. Tara appeared behind her as she stared at what was her living quarter. "Oh ... you are *so* lucky," Tara said. Lily didn't blame her for having a twinge of jealousy in her voice.

Lily's room was huge, with an enormous window overlooking the entire elfin city. There was an awesome-looking video game console with at least fifty games on a nearby table. A giant glass TV dominated a quarter of the living room. The bedroom contained a posh queen-sized bed. Lily and Tara went into the kitchen to find a polished dining table, a chandelier, and a sparkling granite countertop. Lily opened the fridge to find thousands of foods stacked neatly on shelves. Pizza, ice cream, soda and candy made up only one-tenth of the varieties of foods. "Wow," Lily commented, "this is nice." "You think?" Tara asked.

Lily checked out Tara's room and found that was just as amazing as her room. She grabbed a bowl of salad and a can of Coke from her fridge and ate her lunch. For the first time, she realized just how hungry she was. Lily gobbled down the salad and added a yogurt to her meal. Then, yawning, she collapsed on her bed and fell asleep instantly, for once not worrying about dwarves.

Chapter 28

More dwarves!

Lily got out of bed and stretched. For the first time in a long while, she had gotten a good night's sleep. She made some pancakes and munched down breakfast. Soon she could greet Stacy, Tara, and Jake and start the day. There was a lot of work to do, setting things right, taking care of the dwarves, and possibly even building a new eastern tower. *At least there are no more dwarves attacking us for now*, Lily thought.

BANG! Startled, Lily dropped her glass of milk. The sounds of people screaming could be heard. Through the gigantic window, she could see a whole new army of dwarves marching over the northern wall rubble and into the central tower. Tara rushed out of her room. "Lily, hurry up!" she yelled. "Oh, no," Lily moaned, "more dwarves?"

PART 2:

THERESA, THE QUEEN

Chapter 29

A city in chaos

Lily groaned and grabbed her sword. "What kind of wake-up call is a bunch of dwarves?" she demanded. "It's a very effective one," Tara said. Snatching up her loudspeaker, Lily rushed out of her room and ran down the hallway.

Elves were running all over the place, screaming and basically making everything much harder for everyone else to save the world. Jake ran over. He had gotten a new sword. Judging from the cuts on his hands he had already joined the fight. Lily yelled into her loudspeaker, "*STACY, WHERE ARE YOU? WE NEED YOU! OW - EVERYBODY, WILL YOU JUST STOP MOVING FOR ONE SECOND?*" as elves jostled her and nearly knocked her over. The dwarves screamed obscenities and shook their weapons, terrorizing hysterical citizens. "Dang it! Freaking stupid crappy-" Jake yelled as he ran into the chaos. "Language, people!" Stacy appeared behind Tara. "Okay, now hopefully we're ready to fight. Right, guys?" Tara said. "I suck at fighting," Stacy whined. "Nonsense, everybody can fight," Tara chided, "now, come on!"

Lily knocked the first dwarf out with a well-aimed punch as the others jumped into action. Suddenly a group of about one hundred dwarves raised their swords and charged straight at them.

As if they weren't already occupied and outnumbered already. Lily brought up her own sword.

Chapter 29: A city in chaos

Watching Jake fight with his sword probably saved Lily's life. She barely managed to defend herself with the sword techniques that Jake used. The best offense maneuver she could do was cut the blade off a dwarf's sword, which worked well enough. Jake shouted, "Take that! And that! And-oh, run away, already!" as he hacked away with his own sword. Lily feared that it wouldn't be long before the dwarves put forward the more dangerous weapons into the battle. "Tara, Stacy, evacuate the elves!" she yelled. She tossed Tara her loudspeaker and ducked to avoid a jumping dwarf with a club. Tara rolled and smashed the loudspeaker - which thankfully didn't break - over a dwarf's head before ordering the elves to evacuate. Stacy had vanished somewhere else among the crowd. A very fat and small dwarf waddled towards Lily with a small blade in his hands. Lily kicked him over and yelled in pain. The dwarf felt like a bag of cement - heavy and *very* painful to kick.

"Lily, get some more weapons!" Tara said. Lily dodged another jumping dwarf and ran for the armory, pushing her way through elves and dwarves with her sword in its sheath. She grabbed a dagger for herself, a sword for Tara, and a dart gun for Stacy. Lily also snatched up a bag of ultra-explosive grenades. Throwing the sword to Tara, she ran outside the northern tower, where two thousand more dwarves awaited her. "Hey, Jake, catch!" she yelled. She dug a grenade out of the bag and lobbed it at Jake, who promptly caught it, pressed the detonation button, and batted it away with his sword, baseball style. The grenade sailed right into the middle of the dwarves and exploded.

BOOM! Dwarves flew everywhere. Ten dwarves crashed into Jake, who fell over. Lily drew both of her blades and started fighting the remaining dwarf crowd. Turns out, she wasn't too bad with the dagger. It worked wonderfully if she used the dagger to block attacks and her sword to attack. The *Alpha 201* appeared above in the sky. Lily could see Stacy sitting inside the cockpit. A ladder dropped and Lily grabbed one rung, holding on tight as the ladder retracted into the spaceship. "Welcome aboard the *Alpha 201*," Stacy announced. "I got you this," Lily said. She handed Stacy the dart gun. Stacy pressed a button on the piloting console and part of the front windshield slid back. "Open the window and chuck a few grenades out for me," Stacy said. Lily yanked open the side window and began dropping grenades on the dwarves' heads as the aircraft rose higher into the sky.

Various weapons sailed through the open window, forcing Lily to duck. Stacy let go of the driving wheel with one hand and raised the dart gun. Lily shrieked and slammed the window shut as a dwarf's grenade exploded against the glass.

Bang! "What the crap was *that*?" Lily said.

There was an empty grenade shell lodged in one of the now-damaged engines, sparking and sizzling. Stupid dwarves. Lily was thrown across the spaceship as it tilted crazily. The other engine exploded as a fragment of the grenade shell flew into it. Stacy's dart gun slid across the piloting console and flew out of the open windshield. "Abort the *Alpha 201*. I repeat, abort the *Alpha 201*," Stacy said over the intercom. She steered the aircraft to the left as it tumbled towards the ground. Unbuckling their seatbelts, Stacy and Lily jumped out of the aircraft as it nose-dived into the ground with a BANG and a giant fireball. A whole platoon of dwarves was crushed under the ten tons of flaming spaceship.

Lily and Stacy got to their feet and pushed their way through the dwarves. Tara ran up to them. "Was that your spaceship?" she asked accusingly at Stacy. "Yep," Lily and Stacy said in unison. "Well, we've got no time to lose." Jake appeared behind Tara. "I've found a tunnel close to the dwarves."

Chapter 30

The gray mist

Lily, Stacy, Tara, and Jake crawled through the tunnel. It didn't have a ridiculously low ceiling like the exit tunnel from the dwarf-packed stone chamber, but it was pretty darn close. The metal tunnel led to a simple room made of rock, with no light except for the daylight streaming through a window with no glass. A metal grate was attached to the window. In the center of the room there was a small box. Sword raised, Lily approached the box.

Lily Claire. Lily froze. A female voice resonated from the container. *I have been waiting for you.* Jake stared at the talking box. "Should I destroy it?" "Wait," Lily said. The voice laughed. *Jake Iander, be lucky I haven't destroyed your precious city yet.* A tiny chute opened at the front of the box. Faster than Lily could react, a misty cannonball shot out of the box and hit Stacy, who collapsed.

Tara yelled, "Stacy!" as Jake prepared his sword. Stacy suddenly gasped and sat up. "Stacy! Are you okay?" Lily ran to Stacy, but stumbled back as she turned to face her. Her eyes glowed. Stacy had an amused look on her face. But when she spoke, the voice was not hers. *Ah, Lily. So foolish and brave. What will you do when your planet is destroyed?* It was the voice from the talking box.

"Stacy, what ..." Tara's voice had become small. "Stop this!" Jake shouted. Stacy laughed. *My power is limitless. There is nothing that can stop me.* Stacy lunged forward faster than anyone could react and pressed her hand against Jake's forehead. He crumpled. Stacy smiled. *My plan shall work. Soon the universe shall be mine!* Jake got to his feet. He tilted his head. *If you choose, Lily, you may leave with that fool Tara.* Tara raised her sword, but Lily murmured, "Stop." Tara ran towards Jake, ready to strike. "Stop!" Lily yelled.

It was too late. Jake dodged Tara's blade and tapped her arm. Right before she collapsed, she looked at Lily, like: *You could've been faster.* Jake and Stacy waited patiently until Tara sat up, gasping, and joined the rest of them. It was then Lily remembered that she had a bag full of ultra-explosive grenades attached to her belt. Now all she had to do was figure out how to detonate them without hurting her friends and herself. "First of all, you don't know me," she told the box. Tara spread her hands. *Lily, everyone knows you as the human girl who caused the elves to lose the war.* "Oh, yeah? I've got just the weapon for you." Lily kept her hand on her belt. Jake growled. *No weapon is possibly enough to stop me. Which of my minions will you attack? I am one being and I am indestructible.* "What about this?" Lily brought out a grenade and pressing the detonation button, spiked it like she was playing volleyball (with grenades) between Jake's feet, in the hope the grenade wasn't *super* explosive.

BOOM! Jake flew backward and crashed into Tara and Stacy. Stacy slammed into a wall as Lily swung her sword at the box. Four more chutes opened up on the box and tendrils of mist slithered out, solidifying into metal tubes. Her sword clanged off the first one. The tubes sprouted swords and closed in around Lily. She barely managed to deflect the blades with her sword and dagger. Jake and Tara stepped forward. Stacy moved to one side so now that they formed a loose semicircle. *How long will it take before you are captured?* Stacy smiled. Tara and Jake brought their swords down on Lily. Lily batted both of them away with her sword and dagger and kicked the box backward into the wall. Stacy, Jake, and Tara shuddered. Lily stepped sideways, getting ready to hit the box again. *You fool!* Stacy screeched and grabbed Lily, shoving her into the wall opposite from the talking evil box. Jake snarled uncertainly. *That was enough power to knock out fifty people! How are you still conscious?* Lily realized that even though Stacy had touched her, she hadn't collapsed. "Like I said," she replied, her voice shaking slightly, "you don't know me."

Jake shouted with rage and threw his sword at Lily, who ducked as the metal blade impaled the wall. *Destroy her!* Tara yelled. Lily held her sword and dagger together and leaped forward. *No!* Jake shouted. Dodging the box's sword arms, which were flailing wildly, Lily drove her two blades into the box and it fell apart into a pile of metal scraps.

Stacy screamed in anger. She and Jake and Tara turned to face Lily. They spoke as one, a voice filled with hate: *I will have my revenge. Watch. Wait. Listen.* All of them collapsed.

Chapter 31

The freeze dome

Lily inched forward, clutching her sword and dagger. Stacy sat up, groaning. "Why am I on the floor?" she asked. Lily helped her to her feet. "Do you remember anything?" she asked. Jake looked at the broken box. "The box was talking, and then, um … that's all I remember." "I'm pretty sure that the box was in one piece," Tara said. The room they were in rumbled. "Guys, we should get out of here, like, *now*," Lily said. They exited the room as it collapsed with a BANG and a lot of dust.

***

Jake wanted a memory refresh.

He wanted to know how he had ended up on the floor with his sword in the wall. He remembered wanting to destroy the metal box and then the box had started talking … saying something about how he was lucky it hadn't destroyed his city.

He was so confused. How could a small box destroy the elfin city? But, seriously, maybe the talking box had a knack for joking about possible impending doom.

They crawled out of the tunnel. Lily turned to Jake. "You don't remember *anything*?" "No," he said. "Nothing bad happened, right?" "Yeah," Lily muttered. "*Nothing bad happened.*"

Stacy stopped in her tracks. "Wait, time out," she said. "Seriously, Lily, what happened?" Lily fell silent for a count of ten before she spoke.

"The box ... it launched gray mist through you, Stacy, and then you started talking with its voice ..." Lily said. Tara blinked. "Are you sure that happened? Because I'm *positive* I don't remember *that*." "I wish it never happened," Lily agreed. "But, yeah, I'm sure."

Jake thought about how Lily had managed to yank his sword out of the wall right before they exited the room. "How did my sword end up in the wall?" "You threw it," Lily replied. "Okay," Jake said, "so I somehow threw my sword into the wall without even knowing?" "Yep," Lily replied. "What did the voice sound like?" Tara said. "The voice was female. When the box spoke, the voice echoed around the whole room," Lily answered. "I only know one person who would be like that. Her name's Theresa. She's the queen of the dwarves, but she's been locked in a prison for decades. She's known to project her voice when she wants to," Jake speculated. "How?" Lily marveled. "Magic. Her family was born with the powerful gift," he replied.

"So ... the box isn't going to turn us into freaky zombies again?" Stacy asked hopefully. "It shouldn't," Tara said, "unless a heap of metal pieces can somehow survive having a room falling on top of it."

Lily sighed. "Well, I guess we'll have to go back and fight the dwarves." Suddenly Jake said, "Wait." The others turned to face him. "Where's the fighting?" he asked. He was right. The air was unnaturally silent. Lily ran to the edge of the hill where the tunnel opening had been placed. Both armies stood still. In the distance, a new dwarf army was gathering. Jake peered into the sky and saw a thin gray dome covering the elfin city, like a picture put through a filter. A *freeze dome*, he thought. Confused, Stacy took one step over the hill and froze completely in her tracks.

"Stacy!" Lily cried. Tara grabbed one of Stacy's hands, which poked out of the freeze dome. She tried to pull her out of the dome without success. Stacy remained frozen, looking blankly down the hill. Tara tripped and nudged Stacy forward. "Stacy only can be moved farther into the dome," Jake realized. Lily reached out as far as she dared and pulled a stick out of Stacy's pant pocket. "What is that?" Jake asked. "A metal stick," Lily replied sarcastically. "Tara, push Stacy forward as much as you can." Tara shoved Stacy five feet down the hill. "Stand back, everyone," Lily warned. She aimed the stick at the freeze dome and pulled a yellow metal jutting out on the bottom back.

BZZZTT! The stick made a sound like a bug zapper as lightning shot out, washing over the dome and weakening its power. Elves and dwarves began to move in very slow motion. Stacy started to turn around. Lily yanked a red stick back and fire shot out, joining the lightning and turning off the freeze dome completely. Stacy finished turning around. "Wha - Lily, why do you have my sword?" Lily tossed the metal stick back. Yells of confusion and battle filled the air as elves and dwarves continued fighting. "We have to stop them!" Tara said. Jake pulled his sword out of his sheath. "Let's go, then!" Lily yelled. They charged down the hill.

Stacy fired her dangerous metal stick into the dwarf army as Lily lobbed grenades about every ten seconds. Dwarves turned in confusion and were blown into the air. Tara did a review of how to properly whack a dwarf with a sword. She swung her blade and cut down five dwarves at once. A dwarf charged her with his own sword raised, but

Tara stepped on the blade, forcing it up to its hilt in the ground. He struggled to yank his blade from the dirt. As she prepared to take down another fifty dwarves, a voice shook the ground.

Chapter 32

Theresa speaks

ELVES. Lily stopped in her tracks as the familiar voice traveled over the ground. *I WILL SPARE YOU AND YOUR CITY FOR A PRICE. GIVE ME THE HUMAN GIRL.* "Theresa, where are you?" Lily yelled. "Show yourself!" The queen of the dwarves laughed. *WHY WOULD I BE FOOLISH ENOUGH TO REVEAL MYSELF? YOU KNOW THAT YOUR FRIENDS ARE ALREADY OUTNUMBERED. SURRENDER AND I WILL SAVE YOU FROM YOUR DOOM.* Lily looked around uncertainly. All around her, elves and dwarves had stopped fighting, listening to Theresa's evil words. Several elves were whispering in one another's ears, pointing at Lily.

Stacy appeared behind Lily. "Theresa, we know you're there!" she called. *STACY, IT'S SO GOOD TO SEE YOU AGAIN. I WILL SPARE YOU FROM SEEING THE DESTRUCTION OF YOUR FRIENDS AND THEIR CITY. HOW LONG WILL IT BE UNTIL YOU ARE UNDER MY CONTROL AGAIN?* "Attack the dwarves!" Tara ordered. The elf fighters paid her no attention. *CAPTURE THE GIRL,* the queen of the dwarves thundered, *AND YOUR HOME WILL NOT BE HARMED.* The elves snapped out of their trance and started to move again.

Half of the elf army was concentrating on battling the dwarves, but the other half was trying to grab Lily. Hundreds of elves were tripping over one another to give Lily over to Theresa. Lily held up her sword and dagger in a defensive X. "Get back!" she screamed. She kicked the closest elf back into the crowd. Another elf from behind raised his sword and began to force some of the elves back. When he turned Lily saw ... Jake.

As she was preparing to thank Jake, she realized that something was wrong. This elf looked like Jake, but he was dressed a little differently and was also taller. "Parker, how many times do I have to tell you to stop trying to save our lives?" Jake complained, somewhere else near Lily. Jake's older brother grinned. "He doesn't know anything," he whispered. He turned to face Jake, who was about twenty feet away. "Don't worry, baby brother! I'll always get the enemies before you!" he called back. Parker jumped back into the elf crowd before Jake could reach him with his sword. Nearby, Tara was fighting sword to sword with another elf, her sword flashing as it knocked the blade out of the other elf's hands. She kicked the weaponless elf back into the crowd.

Stacy ran over. "Don't trust any elf that looks dangerous!" she called. *All of the elves look dangerous*, Lily thought. "Lily, back away!" Jake said. Lily backed up and the crowd pressed forward. She threw an ultra-explosive grenade high in the air, and it soared in a graceful arc towards the ground. When it exploded, it knocked most of the elves in the front row off their feet. The dwarves sent a firebomb into the sky. It detonated in midair and a wave of fire roared over the elves.

Elves ran around in confusion. Several had been hit by the fire and were stumbling around, wailing. Tara was sitting on the ground, hugging her leg to herself. Lily ran over and Tara said, "Ow." "Can you walk?" Lily asked. Tara glared at her. "Oh, good question. I've just been knocked over by a dwarf bomb, and I landed on my leg. You think I can walk?" she demanded. "Yes." Lily helped Tara get to her feet. Tara sat back down near the base of the hill, away from the battle. "Give me five to ten minutes and I'll be as good as new," she promised. Lily left her on the grass and ran over to Stacy. "Any luck?" she asked. "Nah," Stacy replied. Lily punched an elf in the face. "Any ideas about how we can stop this?" "Nah," Stacy replied.

Stacy hefted her metal stick and fired a crackling bolt of pure electricity into the dwarf army. "I wouldn't get close to the dwarves if I were you," she said. "You do *not* know what dwarf breath smells like." Lily shuddered with revulsion. Jake yelled, "Go away, you stupid dwarves!" Lily threw a grenade into the dwarf crowd. "You should hide before anyone spots you," Stacy advised. "There!" an elf shrieked, pointing at Lily. "Too late," Lily grumbled. She gripped her sword and dagger and shouted, "Your city will not be destroyed! Theresa, the queen of the dwarves, is planting lies into your mind. Get back!"

For one blissful moment, the crowd of elves obeyed, wavering uncertainly. Then they came back to their senses and ran forward. "Get into the dwarf crowd!" Tara called. Lily stepped sideways and ran into the dwarf army. The crowd stopped their chase, screaming in rage. She ran deeper into the dwarves, sprinting over rocks and whacking dwarves, avoiding their bad breath.

BOOM! BOOM! Lily looked to her left. The dwarves had brought catapults with them. They were firing huge clumps of dirt towards the elves. A dwarf ran into Lily and shoved her out of the crowd. A dirtball sailed towards her. Lily slashed upward with her sword and it split neatly in half before crumbling to dust on either side of her. Tara stood up and picked up her own sword. She ran into the dwarves like a lawn mower. Elves scattered as dirt slammed into the ground. Jake ducked as a dwarf nearly smacked into his head, launched into the air by a clump of dirt. Lily spotted a small ledge over a tiny cave on the side of the hill, hidden from the elves' and the dwarves' view. "Guys, let's go!" she yelled. Tara, Stacy, Jake, and Lily made their way behind the hill and under the ledge.

"So," Jake said, "what's the plan?" "I don't have one," Lily replied. "Well, that's just great," Tara grumbled. The vines hanging above the ledge began to swing in the air, but there was no wind to move them. Lily rested her hand on the hilt of her sword. "Guys, there's something wrong-"

The vines whipped around, lashing themselves together and extending so that they attached to the ground. Tara hit them with her sword, but in clanged off. In the suddenly dim light, Lily could see screws on the vines. "I think we're trapped," she noted. Stacy yelped in surprise. "Why is the wall doing something weird?"

They whipped around to find that the wall was rippling like a mirage, rumbling loudly. A small opening formed in the middle. Theresa's voice echoed around the area. *I will only let the human in.*

"I *really* hate that voice," Lily grumbled. She said to the others, "Stay here. Try to find a way to get out." She headed into the tunnel.

Chapter 33

A look into a prison

The tunnel opened into a small cave. There was barely enough room for Lily to stand. She got to her feet. *Welcome*, Theresa said. "I'm alone in this stupid cave," Lily said, "so why don't you show yourself?" The voice hissed. *Take a look at my prison, and you shall see.* "Prison?" Lily asked. She stumbled backward as images flooded into her mind.

A majestic castle towered over Lily's head. The light inside was very faint, so she could only see the bars over the giant windows and door. Lily glanced to her right and saw a figure sitting on a throne, no doubt Theresa. The queen of the dwarves said, "You see? Here is my prison. I am trapped. Slowly I make my way out of this place. And then I will find the person who imprisoned me." "What do you mean?" Lily asked. A small cloud of gray magic made its way to the barred door, coming from Theresa's faintly lit fingers. The glowing fog smashed into the bars curling around them, and the metal began to corrode and bend. The mist retracted and the bars mended themselves. Theresa growled in frustration. "This place seems pretty comfy, huh?" Lily asked. "Why don't you just stay here?" "Oh, I could. But fifty years in a prison gets boring."

"Why don't you turn the lights on?" Lily suggested. "Then we can have a proper conversation." "Oh, no, Lily," Theresa purred, "I won't have you seeing me until you are here for real." "Then how about you tell me why you want to destroy the elves so badly?" Lily said. Theresa laughed. "Isn't it obvious? The elves have been the dwarves' enemy for thousands of years, ruling most of the land and setting up limited laws. Their peace treaty didn't change anything. I want to stop them once and for all and allow the dwarves to rule the universe for eternity. They should know what it is like to lose, to be barred out." "Sounds like a good plan," Lily agreed. "Except for the fact that I do *not* like the dwarves."

Those cold eyes turned to look at her again. "I always love my plans for universal domination. But I need you, my dear, to help make this work. Without you, the elves will have no hope. Already I have convinced them to capture you for me. Ha! Those people will do anything to save their stupid city." The queen struck at the door's metal bars again, hitting them with so much force that they nearly snapped in two. Lily faintly saw Theresa reclining in her chair. "Yes," Theresa murmured. "Soon I will be free." She waved her hand at Lily. "Be gone."

Lily opened her eyes. She was no longer standing in the giant castle. The tiny cave was in its place. Lily crawled back through the tunnel.

Stacy helped her out of the tunnel. "How long did I go?" Lily asked. "About twenty to twenty-five minutes," Stacy replied. The metal vines covering the ledge slid back. Lily must've looked bad because Tara glanced back at her. "What happened, Lily? You look weird." "I'm fine," Lily said. "Are you sure?" Stacy asked. "Yeah, I'm fine," she insisted. No one asked her any more questions as Lily went out of the ledge.

***

Chapter 33: A look into a prison

The battle below them was worse than ever. Stacy stared at the colossal mayhem that had built over the last thirty minutes. *How will we ever stop this?* She thought. Lily drew her sword and dagger. She still seemed distracted. Stacy decided it was best not to disturb Lily while she was thinking. Tara sprinted down the hill and charged straight into battle. Lily tossed a grenade into the air and used the flat side of her sword to smack it down into the dwarf crowd.

The elves seemed to be having trouble fighting, halfway to follow Theresa's words, halfway to smacking the enemy. "Their general is not here," Jake realized. "He has either fled the battle or is unable to fight." "Then who's the next best general?" Lily asked. "How am I supposed to know?" he demanded. He went to the top of the hill and gazed down at the chaos below. Raising his sword, he yelled, "Listen up, people! Go and GAH!" A shield sailed up and hit him in the face, and Jake went down. Stacy groaned in exasperation and kicked a dwarf into his own brethren, knocking down six more of the little people (or maybe a more scientific term would be *vertically challenged*). Dwarves fell down about every five minutes, and they didn't get up, probably because they were in danger of being trampled by the other million bloodthirsty dwarves running down the hill. So if I were you, I wouldn't technically call it a *success.*

To make matters worse, someone screamed, "There she is!" and the crowd of elves who had listened to Theresa's words surrounded Lily. "Beware!" Lily yelled. "Take one step forward and you will be forced to fight the dwarves. There's no going back." "Listen to them," Stacy chimed in, "and don't fight Lily, fight the dwarves!" "What in the world are you people *doing*?" Jake shouted as several elves lobbed grenades up at him. He batted them away with his sword and they exploded in a massive shockwave, sending him flying backward.

Lily took one glance up at the hill, momentarily distracted. The crowd of elves took their chance and surged forward. Tara leaped toward them and began to knock out the first few people. Lily tossed a grenade over their heads and pulled Tara out of the way as it exploded in the middle of the crowd. Elves on the sides were suddenly shoved forward as others crashed into them. Stacy ran around, calling into the crowd, "Your armor is loose! That one called you stupid! Look out, there's an armed dwarf behind you!" causing confusion as elves turned around or started arguing with others.

Tara shouted, "Come on!" Jake ran down the hill followed Lily and Stacy to where Tara was standing. "What's the plan?" Lily asked. "There's a conference room where we can actually *make* a plan," Tara offered. Stacy said, "You three go. I'll try to stop the others from reaching you." She dodged a jumping dwarf and disappeared into the angry mob of elves.

Chapter 34

The creepy gray mist appears once again

Lily, Jake, and Tara made their way through the crowd until they reached the northern tower. Entering, Tara went to a hallway and led the others to a door. Lily pushed it open.

Two stone columns stretched up, rising twenty feet high from the ceiling to the floor. Jake circled the room. "This would be a good place to make a plan," he said. "Yeah," Lily agreed. "We finally get a place to rest and-"

Behind them, Tara hissed.

Lily whipped around. Tara stared at them, and as though she were in a trance, took a step forward. The Gray Mist Lady had come back. "Was this what you were talking about?" Jake whispered. "Yes," Lily said. *I would have you in my control, Jake*, Tara said, *but I am saving my energy for the final break.* Tara's eyes sparkled dangerously. "Uh, can you let Tara go?" Jake prompted. Tara looked at him. *If someone asked you to release a prisoner you have just caught, would you oblige?* "No," Jake admitted. Lily whispered, "Distract her." Jake cleared his throat. "So, Theresa," he said. "Any luck with your plan?" Theresa laughed. *My plan is going along well, thank you very much. But I have a little side errand. I know you will not leave without Tara. On a normal day, I would have never let her go. But I am in a good mood. I'll give you a small test.*

A small round table erupted from the stone floor. A tiny red button was perched on it. "The button stops your power momentarily, doesn't it?" Lily said. "If we press it, Tara will be free." *Yes,* Theresa said. Jake's eyes flickered at the button. He sheathed his sword. Lily put her dagger away, but she left her sword out. *Go and get the button,* Theresa teased. *I would like to see you try.* Jake lunged for the button.

A smile appeared on Tara's face as she thrust out her hand. Gray mist flowed from her fingers. The glowing tendrils wrapped themselves around Jake, sending him flying backward into one of the columns, where they lashed him tight against the stone. *I think I like this room,* Theresa said. *Two columns. Two troublesome people to tie them to.* She stretched out her other hand and more gray fog pushed Lily against the other column. Tara watched them with an amused look on her face as they struggled against their bonds.

"I can't reach my sword!" Jake said. Lily turned her own sword in her hand so the tip pointed upwards. As the blade touched the mist the gray fog sizzled. The sword seemed to be drinking in the evil magic. Lily carefully cut through the mist and it disappeared. Tara stood up, growling. *You dare oppose me?* Theresa snarled. "Press the button!" Jake said. Lily started towards the small round table, but Tara stepped in her way. *You will come with me,* she said. The queen sent more gray mist at her. "Get the button!" Jake yelled as he struggled against his restraints. Lily hesitated as gray fog shot towards her. "PRESS THE BUTTON!" Jake shrieked. Lily leaped over the mist and slammed her fist down on the button. Tara shuddered and blinked.

"What just happened?" Tara blinked in confusion. "Theresa happened!" Jake said. "Now get me out of here!" Still perplexed, Tara slashed through the mist with her sword.

Chapter 34: The creepy gray mist appears once again

"We need to get out of here," Lily said. "Give me a second ..." Jake sat down on the floor and rubbed his arms. "The button would stop Theresa from attacking us only for a minute," Lily insisted. As if on cue, glowing gray tendrils flowed from the wall opposite them and raced forward. They ran out of the room, Lily slamming the door behind them. Slicing a lamp off the hallway wall, she tucked as many explosive grenades as she could into the lamp shade, kicked open the door, tossed the grenades inside, and quickly closed the door.

"Back away!" Lily ordered. They hugged the wall as the explosion rocked the floor. The room door was nearly blasted off its hinges. Silence filled the air. Lily was just starting to think, *Dang, it actually worked*, but suddenly gray mist seeped out from under the door. "Theresa is *not* happy," Tara noticed. They ran for their lives as Theresa's voice screamed in anger.

Chapter 35

The crowd goes wild

They raced each other out of the northern tower. Tara ducked as a stray arrow sailed over her head and pushed her way deeper into battle. Stacy had apparently gotten a sword because she was sparring with a fat dwarf. Tara vaulted over her head and slammed the heels of her shoes into the back of the dwarf's head. "What took you so long?" Stacy demanded. "I've already punched about a thousand dwarves in the face." "Oh, I was just having Theresa whirling around in my head," Tara replied. As she spoke, she wondered how she remembered Theresa in her head. Then she realized, when she had suddenly been frozen, there was a voice speaking in her mind: *You're mine, now.*

Tara snapped back to attention, kicked a dwarf's *gluteus maximus*, and said, "We can talk later, but right now we don't have much time!" Stacy brushed her hair back from her face and returned to her role of an awesome butt kicker. Jake ran at the dwarves, but suddenly he fell back like he'd just slammed into something. He got to his feet, dazed, and began pounding the air. Tara looked hard and saw a shimmering force field surrounding Jake like a small cage. Stacy leaped at a dwarf and flew backward, sliding off another force field. The same thing happened to Lily. Tara carefully took one step forward and bumped into an invisible wall, no doubt another force field cage.

Gray fog gathered outside of Tara's cage, taking on the form of a panther. The glowing animal looked disdainfully at Tara but didn't attack. *I would like to destroy you, but I want you to watch the end of your city*. "Theresa," Tara said. "Only one person has a voice that ugly." The panther bared its fangs. *If you want to live, stop talking. Watch your people fall under my power.*

The panther took off into the crowd. It dodged the dwarves with ease, passing through the elves. They fell to the ground, shaking violently and clutching their heads in agony. Tara drew her sword. She hacked at the force field and the blade passed right through it. Perplexed and frustrated, she attempted to pull the sword out of the shimmering dome. The force field seemed to suck at the blade, resisting Tara like a game of tug of war. It took all of her effort to yank it out. The blade made an impressive squelching sound as it came out. As the last few elves fell, the panther turned to Theresa. *If you wish to be released, I will let you try*. Lightning suddenly arched across Tara's invisible cage.

Tara glanced at Jake, who was trying to pull his sword out of his force field. *A plan would be nice*, she thought. She couldn't get past the force field without being electrocuted, but what other choice did she have? Tara thought of how stupid her plan was. She charged at her cage wall, straight at the panther.

Apparently, Theresa hadn't thought Tara would be so suicidal because she stepped back in surprise. For one second, the lightning flickered out, and Tara took her chance, passing through the cage and charging at the panther. The animal snarled and glared at her with pure hatred as she brought her sword down on it. The panther turned into a cloud of mist that floated away in the wind.

The other force fields went out and Lily came over. "Tara, that was amazing," she said. Tara stared at the elves on the ground, groaning and shuddering. "Our work is not done," she announced. "Well, of *course*, it's not done," Jake said. "I need to find Theresa and punch her out of her stupid palace of a prison." Stacy nodded enthusiastically. "Oh, yes." "Uh, guys, what's going on?" Lily pointed at the dwarves, who were retreating over the hills. Tara watched as a new army rose to meet them – elves, shuddering as they saw her and her friends.

Jake waved his sword in annoyance, which made Stacy back away. "Can Theresa bend that many elves to her will? Please say no." "Yes," Stacy offered. "The crowd goes wild," Lily muttered. Elves began to get to their feet. In a stupor, they stumbled over the grass towards Tara and the others. One grabbed Lily and she screamed, but Jake whacked him and the elf collapsed. "Let's go!" he ordered. The group ran for their lives as the elves wailed in Theresa's voice, *Capture them! Destroy them!*

Chapter 36

The animatronics

They barely made it inside the tower.

As soon as Stacy locked the northern door, elves slammed into it, rattling the doorknob and screaming for their capture. Lily calmly rolled a grenade under the door. "What do we do now?" she asked. "Go to the control room," Stacy answered.

They went into a secret garage behind a hidden door. The whole room was completely empty. Jake stepped forward. "Operation Animatronics, engage," he said. The floor opened and four robot animals rose up on a platform. There was a horse, a bear, a giant snake, and a donkey. The animals looked so real, but Lily knew they were actually robots. Stacy inspected each animal. "They're still in good condition," she announced. Lily went up and rested her hand on the horse's amber back. "Do they move?" she asked. "Yes," Tara answered. "Just climb on," Stacy explained.

Lily swung herself onto the horse's back and instantly it reared up on its hind legs, almost throwing her. She clung on as Stacy climbed on the bear. Tara got the snake, and Jake ended up with the donkey. Tara kicked the snake to life. She dashed out the door and came back two minutes later with a fancy, chariot-like wagon. She attached it to the snake and climbed on. "Everyone good to go?" Stacy called. She yelled, "Open the garage!" and the garage door slid up. The horse, smelling freedom (if a robot horse could smell freedom) bolted out onto the grass. The bear lumbered out slowly and the donkey trotted happily outside. Tara carefully steered the snake onto the grass.

"Let's go, then," Lily said. She kicked the horse's sides with her feet. "Giddy up!" The horse didn't budge. On the bear, Stacy scratched her head. "Oh, right," she said, "they'll only listen to you if you call them by their names." She gave everyone the animals' names. When she came to Tara she frowned. "Oops. I think they forgot to give your snake a name."

Lily held on tight to the horse's soft mane. "Uh, hi there. Can you please go to that crowd?" She pointed at the dwarf army. The horse nickered impatiently. "Can you please go to that crowd, *Foxfire*," Stacy supplied. "Yes, yes," Lily grumbled. She stared at the dwarf army. "Foxfire, go!"

Foxfire bolted forward so fast, Lily nearly tumbled off. Fortunately, the last time she'd ridden a horse was only two or three years ago ... which meant she didn't have much experience, which was rather unfortunate. The dwarves were ten miles away, but the horse was halfway there in two minutes. A streak of gray and gold rushed past below them. Lily looked at it, confused until she saw Tara in her fancy wagon of a chariot being pulled along by the snake.

Lily urged Foxfire forward and he leaped into the battle, scattering dwarves. A dwarf ran towards them with a small but deadly-looking cannon. He aimed and fired a flaming projectile at them. Foxfire whinnied derisively and shot away as the projectile exploded in a miniature mushroom cloud close by. Lily sliced a dwarf's weapon in half as the spear sailed by her face. Trevor the donkey brayed in protest at the dwarves and kicked them with his hind legs. There was a line of dwarves that rippled like a wave, the unnamed snake slithering below them as Tara flattened herself on its back. The snake hissed and with a flick of its tail, pulverized a dwarf cannon.

Foxfire knocked dwarves over like bowling pins, sending weapons flying. A shadow loomed over them. Lily looked up just in time to see Geiger squash a dozen dwarves. The bear strode away triumphantly with Stacy on top. Nearby, Tara yelled, “Find Theresa!” Lily leaned close down towards Foxfire’s head and whispered the command in his ear. “Foxfire, find Theresa.”

Chapter 37

The hidden palace

The horse snorted and instantly changed direction, turning right. Out of the corner of her eye, Lily saw Geiger bear right (pardon the pun) chasing her. The grizzly picked up speed until Stacy was right next to Lily. Foxfire shook his head in protest as Geiger sniffed him inquisitively. "Sorry," Stacy said, "I don't think Geiger likes Foxfire; she's never seen him before." "Don't mention it," Lily said.

As they rode on, a strange fog rose from the ground, obscuring almost all vision. Lily's horse didn't seem to be bothered by the grayish fog. Foxfire surged on over the ground. The yells of battle faded away.

Ten minutes later the mist seemed to deepen ever so slightly. Lily started to get tired. Stacy said, "I think we're almost there." Lily stared at the mist. "That makes sense. If this place feels more dangerous, we are definitely close. Stacy pointed up. "I think the fog is thinning. I can see the sky." A gray haze that might have been the sky shimmered above the fog. But the fog was too thick to see anything. "There's something wrong ..." Lily warned. Now she knew they were close, by the 'sky'. The gray mist gathered in front of her, forming an arrow that was unmistakably pointing down. Foxfire slowed down, looking at the hovering arrow. "Stop," Lily said to Stacy. "Lily, what's wro-" "Geiger, stop!" Lily commanded.

Chapter 37: The hidden palace

One second later and it would have been too late for Stacy and her bear. The gray mist parted in front of them, revealing a twenty-foot chasm that seemed to have no bottom. Geiger stumbled to a stop just in time, Stacy hanging on tight to avoid getting thrown. The gray arrow rippled, forming the word, *forward*. "Theresa is on the other side of the gap!" Lily said. "I don't think crossing the gap is a good idea!" Stacy replied. Lily slashed the mist word to nothing with her sword. Foxfire and Geiger went crazy, howling and snapping at the chasm. "We have to go over," Lily said. "Over what?" a voice asked.

Jake appeared behind them, perched on a donkey. "Trevor was acting a little strange and he bolted in your direction," he explained. Trevor trotted closer to the giant gap. "Theresa's on the other side," Stacy said. Jake swore. "Holy cow, you're going to cross *that*?" "It's the only way," Lily said. Trevor suddenly backed up and raced towards the gap. "Whoa, boy, OH NO!" Jake screamed as the donkey leaped right over the edge of the chasm. Geiger did the same, jumping over the edge with Stacy screaming in terror. Foxfire neighed uncertainly. "It's okay," Lily assured, though she was sure nothing was okay. "Jump," she said. After hesitating for a second, Foxfire galloped toward the chasm edge at full speed and jumped.

For five seconds of horror, Lily was sure they weren't going to make it. Then she was jolted forward as Foxfire landed on the other side. Geiger roared. Lily saw a palace, towering over them. "A hundred bucks that's Theresa's prison," she said. "I'm not taking that bet," Jake said.

All three animals suddenly stiffened and fell on their sides, sending Stacy and the others tumbling off. "What's wrong with them?" Stacy cried. Jake shot to his feet, sword in hand. "Theresa's here!" he yelled. "Run for the palace and-"

A gray tendril of mist wrapped around Jake's waist, pulling him screaming into the sky. Lily slashed uselessly through the other mist strings as they wrapped around her and Stacy, dragging them high above the palace. The mist carried them through a roof compartment, dropping them in what must've been the throne room.

Lily recognized the room immediately because it was the room Theresa had shown her in the vision. Strangely, the place seemed deserted. Stacy rubbed her eyes and yawned. "Guys, I'm feeling so tired." Jake also yawned. He fell to the floor. "This is Theresa's prison, all right," he mumbled into the ground. Lily stumbled. "Maybe we should get some rest," she admitted. Stacy and Jake immediately collapsed. Lily was thinking of doing guard duty, but her mind rebelled against the thought. She sank to the floor.

Chapter 38

Theresa makes an appearance

BANG! Stacy sat up. Still half asleep, she slowly got to her feet. "What's that sound?" Lily asked. "I don't know," she replied. Jake stood up. "Well," he said, "we should leave."

As soon as he said that, a tornado of gray mist spun its way to the throne in the middle of the room. It transformed into a woman, no doubt the Queen of Gray mist, Theresa herself. Lily stepped forward. "Hello, Theresa," she said calmly. Stacy could tell she was tempted to lunge at the queen and attack with her sword. But she knew better. A sword and dagger weren't going to do much against pure magic. "Ah," Theresa said. "Let me give you some light."

A sphere of blazing gray light appeared in the queen's hand. Theresa's face was regally beautiful, with dark brown hair and a cold smile that made Lily shudder. Judging from the murderous look in her eyes, she wasn't the type of queen with a boisterous attitude. She was in a simple purple gown and wore a sapphire necklace.

She smiled coldly. "Hello, Lily." "How's your day?" "Very good, thank you very much." Jake coughed. "Uh, sorry to interrupt your conversation, but are you two, like, school chums or something?" Theresa glared at him with malice. "Shut up, you imbecile. I have better things to do than talking to a brainless elf." The queen sent a gray misty lion at Jake, which vaporized within five feet. "Hey, lady," he protested.

"You've had a bad day, and all that, so why don't you let us go?"
"Silence, you fool!" Theresa hissed.

Faster than Stacy could blink, gray mist arched like lightning at Jake's sword, breaking it in half like it was made of tissue paper. Two seconds later more mist slammed into him, sending him crashing into the nearest wall. "OW!" he complained. Theresa studied her hands with satisfaction. "My powers are growing," she noted. "Which means …"

She turned towards the palace doors, and Stacy saw that the chains once binding the doors together were now weakly held with a thin, twisted piece of metal chain. Theresa thrust out her hands and a haze of gray raced at the doors, shattering the chains. She smiled. "Which means that I am almost free. I thank you, Lily, for being so slow coming here."
Stacy swallowed. She waited for Theresa to strike them down or open the palace doors, but the queen didn't move. "Aren't you supposed to be, like, running out through the doors to claim the universe?" she asked. Theresa laughed. "The doors are still closed. I still have to break one more lock. But I do not have the power to achieve my goal. The lock is made of magic." "She's right," Lily said.

Stacy glanced at the doors. Sure enough, there was another haze covering the doors like a transparent blanket. "Then why are we here, anyway?" she demanded. "Don't let her get to the doors," Jake muttered.

Theresa shrugged. "How would you stop me?" Lily drew her sword. The queen sighed. "If you wish, then I will fight you." She sent a torrent of gray mist at Lily, who yelped and rolled to one side. "You are braver than most," Theresa mused. "I'm braver than you, butt face!" Lily yelled.

Unfortunately, that must've hurt the queen's feelings because she snarled and spread her hands. "Duck!" Stacy shouted.

Here's the thing with the word *duck*: many people confuse the bird duck with the term that means *get down, you idiot!* Because of this, Lily ended up looking at her feet, perplexed, instead of hugging the floor. Stacy tackled her as a mist bomb exploded over their heads.

The queen rose out of her throne. "Surrender to me!" she shrieked. "Not happening, Theresa," Stacy grumbled. Another bomb flew at their faces. Before they could actually duck, it detonated, making Stacy fall backward. The queen launched two more bombs at Jake, who was struggling to stay on his feet. Lily intercepted them, whacking them with her sword so they flew right back at Theresa.

"Ack!" Theresa stretched her hands out in front of her, creating a force field so the bombs exploded harmlessly. She glared at her with pure hate. "You're making me waste my energy!" she complained. "Good!" Stacy said. "WHAT?"

Lily pounced and sliced Theresa's throne in half. The queen growled. "You may be winning this war," she said, "but I will have revenge. Already your loved ones are falling in my grasp." Lily raised her dagger, but Jake looked up. "What do you mean?" he asked. Theresa flicked her fingers, making a screen. In it, Lily saw two elves - Parker and Oneida - walking through a tunnel. *I don't know about this, Parker,* Oneida said. *I know he's here,* Parker replied. A gray light flashed at the end of the tunnel. *There he is!* Parker said. He herded his little sister towards the gray light. Stacy watched as Parker's face, set with confidence, suddenly paled. Oneida screamed, and the video dissipated.

"No," Jake said. "That can't be, they were in the war, fighting." Theresa gave him a look of fake sympathy. "Oh, don't worry. That footage was from two hours ago." "*Two hours?*" Jake demanded. The queen didn't answer. Instead, another video popped up on the screen - Tara's mother, racing up a flight of stairs in the city, heading for a sound: Tara screaming for help. The images changed again, showing a sweet little girl that Stacy thought no one would ever think of harming - Sandra, her little sister. As she watched in horror, Sandra wandered through an empty hallway. In front of her, Stacy saw a misty gray version of herself, laughing and leading her deeper down through the corridor. Sandra, giggling, ran forward to hug her, and the screen vanished altogether.

Chapter 39

Return

Stacy yelled, "What have you *done?*" Theresa waved her hand impatiently. "Oh, stop being so glum. They'll all be here in about, hmm ... ten or twenty minutes." Jake moaned, "That sucks." Lily looked at them, concerned. "Uh, thank you for that terrifying presentation, but we really should be going," Lily said. She managed to push the doors open. "Hmm. Fine. Just don't come back," Theresa purred. Lily pushed the others through the doors and shut them. A flash of gray magic glowed between the doors, sealing them.

Foxfire trotted towards Lily. She stroked his mane and he whinnied impatiently, like, *what took you so long, girl?* "I'm all right, Foxfire," she said, though she doubted the others were. Jake climbed onto his donkey. "I guess we go now," he said. "Right," Lily said. She mounted herself on Foxfire's back and he instantly shot off into the gray mist, Geiger and Trevor following close behind. Soon the mist opened up and the battle appeared. Tara met them near the battle.

"Where were you?" she demanded. "And why are Jake and Stacy so pale?" "We met Theresa, and she showed us some crap," Lily said. "What kind of crap?" Tara asked. "She's captured your mother, Tara," Stacy said, "and my sister Sandra, and Parker and Oneida."

Tara gasped. "But how could she possibly-" "Theresa tricked them," Lily said. "Your mom thought you were calling for help." Tara looked ready to run to Theresa's palace and slap her in the face. Her snake hissed. "Please don't go back," Lily said. "We'll find a way together." Tara said something to the snake and they bolted past them. Foxfire chased after her, blocking their way. "There's no point going there," Lily said. Tara's shoulders slumped and she headed back to the dwarves.

Jake tossed what was left of his sword onto the ground. "Tara's right. We should go back." "No," Lily firmly replied. "Jake, stop it. We should ... stay here," Stacy said. She was obviously forcing the words out. She glanced at Lily, and her eyes conveyed a message, repeating itself over and over again: *please let us go back. Please let me save my sister.*

"Change of plans, we'll go there now," Lily relented. Stacy said, "Thank you thank you thank you." "You're welcome," she replied. Jake shouted into the crowd, "Tara! Come on, I changed my mind!" In a flash, Tara was next to them. Lily spurred Foxfire back across the ground, back to Theresa's palace.

Soon they entered Theresa's realm of gray mist. "Stay together!" Lily called to the others. "We should be there in two minutes." Five minutes later the palace hadn't appeared. She urged Foxfire to go faster. "Keep going," she said, "Theresa's prison should be here somewh-"

A wall of gray mist materialized in a flash. Foxfire balked violently to avoid crashing into it. "Calm down!" Lily said into the horse's ear. Then *bam* - a misty gray hologram of Theresa appeared in front of them, glowering. "Come back so soon, haven't you?" Stacy didn't miss a beat. "Hello, Theresa! We'd love to see our families, please." The queen sighed and flicked her hand at them. Gray fog obscured their vision, and Lily felt herself being lifted into the air.

Chapter 40

A family reunion

Theresa dropped them in the throne room.

Jake got to his feet. "Where are the others?" he asked. "Here," Tara said. Theresa drifted - literally since she had turned into mist - over to her newly-repaired throne. She took her time solidifying before settling into her chair. "I will call out the prisoners by family," she said. The queen cleared her throat. "Marissa Aiwa!" A door in the back of the room opened and Tara's mom stood in the doorway. Tara rushed forward and gave her mother a hug.

"Sandra Dana!" Theresa called. A much smaller figure came to the doorway. Stacy cried out in relief and ran over to pick up her baby sister. "Oneida and Parker Iander!" the queen said. Jake's older brother and younger sister ran towards him.

"When can we destroy this place? It's so boring here," Parker said after they had all finished hugging each other. "Soon," Jake promised. "Jake, you've got a scratch on your hand!" Oneida said. She grabbed Jake's hand and inspected it carefully. He squirmed out of her grasp. "I'm fine," he assured. Oneida crossed her arms. "Have you *looked* at yourself lately?" she demanded. "You're covered in dirt, your hair's messy, you've got no weapon ... Mother will be furious at you." "Yes, Mother *will* be furious at me, and I *don't care*," Jake answered. He went over to Stacy, who was cuddling Sandra. She smiled. "Here, you can hold her." She handed the toddler over to Jake.

Jake looked at Sandra as she laughed and wriggled in his arms. She made a funny face and formed a tiny fist. Jake stared cross-eyed at the fist as it punched him in the nose.

"Ow!" Jake gave Sandra back to Stacy and jogged over to his family. "Dude, what's with the new fashion statement?" Parker grinned. Jake looked at him, confused, until Oneida exclaimed, "Jake, you've got a bruise on your face!"

"Ugh." Jake rubbed his nose. "I've only been punched in the nose by a toddler." Parker cracked up. Oneida said, "How could you be so clumsy, Jake?" "Everyone in this family's clumsy," Jake protested. "But you're the most stupid," his sister teased. Jake messed up her cute hair for her troubles.

Over all the commotion Theresa called, "Are you done? I haven't started yet, and I would not like to wait any longer." Jake let go of Oneida. "Wait any longer for what?" The queen smiled. "For you to open the doors, of course. You're my best chance of escaping my prison. If you refuse ... well, I'll just have to destroy you and find someone else." "Thank you, but no," Lily said. "I wanna go home!" Sandra shrieked. Theresa rose out of her throne and everyone stepped backward. A gray tiger appeared in front of her. "Surrender to me!" the queen shrieked. "No!" Jake and Stacy said in unison. Theresa snarled and the tiger lunged.

Tara pushed her mother to one side as the mist tiger leaped right over them, missing by an inch. As it passed by, Tara quickly drew her sword and slashed upward, but the blade went right through. The tiger growled and grew sharp claws, and Jake was sure they weren't mist. The claws gouged deep cuts in the ground as the tiger bared its fangs, deciding who to attack first. Parker whispered, "I'll distract it. Go!" Jake dragged Oneida to one side as his older brother charged the tiger, yelling, "HEY! Over here, teddy!"

The tiger howled and turned as Parker drew his sword and plunged it into the animal. The blade crackled and frost spread up the metal. Parker was forced to drop it. Lily leaped at the queen and sliced the throne in half. "Are you *kidding* me?" Theresa yelled. "It took me five whole minutes to repair that!" "Run!" Stacy shouted as she picked up Sandra. Jake stepped forward and tried to punch the tiger in the face, but his fist passed straight through. Nearby, the queen flicked her hand and the tiger seemed to become more solid. She smiled. "My creation is now permanent. You can try to stop it, but it is intent to bring misery and pain to all of you." Jake began to think. What was the opposite of misery and pain? Oh, right. Happiness and wellness.

Suddenly Jake had a really stupid idea. "Yo, Happy!" he yelled. The tiger turned and growled, *Ruh?* "Yeah," he continued, "you're looking so *cute* and *downright cheerful*!" *Ruh!* The tiger roared and charged him, ignoring the fact that Parker's frost-covered sword was still impaled in its back. Jake dodged it and said, "How you doing, Fluffy? Nice dagger in your back." The tiger roared and Parker's blade shattered into pieces. "Yeah, thanks!" Parker yelled at Jake. Stacy shoved Sandra into Lily's arms, snatched Tara's sword out of her hand, ran forward, and stabbed the tiger right in its glowing gray butt.

Theresa said, "Oh, that's not nice!" A tendril of gray mist grabbed Sandra from Lily. A glowing cage appeared around the toddler, Tara's mother, and Jake's brother and sister. The tiger snarled, confused, like *What just happened?* Gray lightning suddenly coursed through its body and it exploded into mist. "Just because I'm a good mood," the queen said, "I'll give you ten minutes to escape and live." She raised her arms and the walls began to erupt around them.

Chapter 41

The magic labyrinth

"Run!" Jake yelled. "Theresa's creating a labyrinth!" Lily said, "How are we supposed to escape?" The others had been cut off by a giant wall. Jake scratched his head. "If it's just a magical illusion, you should pass right through." Lily pounded on the wall, which was already looking and feeling like solid rock. "Seems like a pretty solid illusion," she noted.

Theresa's voice echoed in the corridor. "You have nine minutes to find your way out of here." The walls swirled around Lily, giving her vertigo. The corridor was now split into three different tunnels. She inspected them without getting too close. "That one," she said, pointing at the tunnel to the right. "It looks the most dangerous." "Right it is," Jake agreed. They ran down the tunnel. Two seconds later white fog spilled into the corridor. "Don't get gassed!" Jake warned. She held her breath and sped deeper into the tunnel. "Seven minutes," Theresa sang. *Shut up*, Lily wanted to say. The fog disappeared and suddenly they were standing in an empty corridor with no visibly dangerous surprises in sight.

Lily frowned. "Something's not right." Jake leaned forward to take a look and a wall of fire nearly burned his face. Lily screamed as he stumbled back. "I am going to punch Theresa in the face," he grunted. He and Lily gradually made progress to the end of the tunnel.

They waited for the wall in front of them to disappear, but it didn't. Lily pounded on the hard stone. "Four minutes!" Theresa said. "Let us go!" Lily yelled. The queen's voice dripped with false sympathy. "Oh, dear. I believe you've come to a dead end." Something caught Lily's eye. To her left, there was a ladder, almost hidden next to the wall. "Let's go!" She grabbed Jake's arm and led him to the ladder.

A roaring sound filled Lily's ears. At the end of the corridor, there was a wall of gray fire that was rapidly gaining on them. She leaped onto the ladder and scrambled up it, Jake following close behind. Jake climbed over the wall as the ladder crumbled to dust underneath him. "Two minutes," Theresa said. Jake yelled something in elfin, and it sounded suspiciously like, "*Will you shut up?*" with an accent. "Wait, how can I understand what you're saying?" Lily asked. "Translator," Jake said. Lily thought of the tiny earpiece she had, which she thought was a communicator.

She looked down and saw a gate, rapidly sliding down. Normally she wouldn't have even thought of going through any door she didn't know about, but she could see wisps of magic floating around inside, so it was obviously very dangerous. *Typical,* Lily thought. She climbed off the wall as fast as she could, hoping that Jake would keep up. They slid under the door right before it clanged shut.

"One minute," Theresa's voice said, "and I'm not going to wait any longer!" "*Mangy birdbrain,*" Jake muttered in elfin. In front of them, there were four doors. Lily opened the leftmost one and Stacy and Tara rushed out. Lily opened the next door. It seemed empty, just a tunnel leading somewhere, but Lily could see the ruins of Theresa's throne and part of her purple dress at the end. "Don't make a sound, of we'll all be destroyed," Lily whispered. Why the sorceress was facing the wrong way, she wasn't sure. But then she saw two other doors in front of the queen - the other two tunnel exits. Lily crept down the corridor as fast as she could.

"Thirty seconds!" Theresa said. Lily rushed forward and tackled her.

"Ack!" The sorceress sat down hard on the floor. Lily got to her feet as the other surrounded her. "Where is everyone else?" she asked. Theresa looked at her innocently. "Oh, I don't know," she said brazenly. "Where are the others?" Stacy pressed. "Maybe Theresa knows," Theresa said, "after all, I am only a hologram." "Liar," Tara said. "I believe the hologram is correct," a voice said.

Theresa stepped into view - the *real* queen, not the person who was apparently a hologram lying on the floor. "But of course, you can't tell who is real," the sorceress said. The Theresa who was lying on the floor smiled and dissolved into mist. "But now you know," the queen said. Jake stepped forward. "Where is my family?" he demanded. Faster than Lily and just about anyone could react; a bow appeared in Theresa's hands. She aimed an arrow at Jake's face. "I am already past my promise," she hissed. "I gave you ten minutes to live, and yet here you are, still alive and unharmed." Tara darted forward and sliced the arrow in half as it sped towards Jake. The queen aimed another arrow at Tara. "None of you could possibly escape my wrath," she said. "Because nobody here is like me, an elf with a magic part in her brain!"

Lily pretended to mishear her. "A magic fart in your brain?" she asked. "Gah!" Theresa's arrow missed Tara by an inch, embedding itself in the wall. "Clean your ears," she said. Lily sighed. "What do you want, Theresa?"

The sorceress beamed at her. "A wonderful question! I want many things." A gray lab coat appeared over Theresa's dress. A misty notepad and pen appeared in her hands, and glasses popped on her face, so she looked just like a college professor - if college professors had magical powers and wanted to take over the world.

She began to take notes. "Let's see. I want to take over the universe. Everyone wants to do that." Theresa adjusted her glasses and continued to write on the notepad. "I want all elves to respect me, preferably by their destruction - oh, wait. Then they wouldn't be there to bow to me. Ha! Hmm ... what else? Oh, right. I would like to get out of this prison once and for all." The queen tore one page from her notepad and tossed it to Lily. Naturally Lily expected it to dissolve into mist, but as the paper floated through the air it solidified into a single sheet of loose-leaf paper. She caught the note and began to read:

Theresa's Greatest Needs

Take over the universe

Destroy all elves/earn eternal respect

Get out of prison

Visit New York for a vacation

Lily finished reading the note and passed it to Stacy, who crammed it in her pocket. Why Theresa liked vacation spots on Earth, she didn't know. A joke? Jake said, "Well, Theresa, um, *Foveae*, your needs are, um, impressive, but you still haven't answered our question. Where are our families?" "Oh, in the basement," the queen replied. "But then, they are guarded by Gwai, one of my best attack dogs, so you have no chance of saving them."

"You have a giant guard named Gwai," Lily said. "How is *Gwai* a proper name?" Two seconds later there was a loud BANG, shaking and cracking the floor. It sounded like something big was tromping underneath them. Lily scanned the room. How were they supposed to get to the basement? The cracks in the floor expanded outwards from a single point. Unfortunately, the spot was directly in front of Theresa, and she didn't want to get that close. Without thinking, Lily felt herself charging the sorceress. Theresa disappeared in a flash of gray as Lily drove her sword into the ground.

Chapter 42

A visit to Gwai

With a groan, a large area of the floor caved in underneath them. Lily managed to hold on to her sword as she fell on the ground below. A large OW echoed through the air. Standing fifteen feet over them, a golden warrior yelled in surprise as chunks of stone bounced off his helmeted head. As the commotion and the dust cleared, Lily decided she needed to get the giant's attention. "Hello!" she said. Gwai didn't move. "YO!" Lily yelled.

"Uh?" Gwai looked down at them. Tara nudged Lily. "Look to your left," she whispered. At the end of the basement, there was a big suspicious cage with a large cloth draped over its sides. It obviously contained the other elves, and Lily didn't like the utter silence radiating from the cage. If only they could reach it ... expect there was a golden giant looking down at them. From the way the blinding light reflected off Gwai's skin, Lily guessed he was metal. She didn't like the idea of having to battle a giant golden warrior.

"I have orders to destroy anyone who comes down here," the giant rumbled. "Yeah, well ..." Lily shrugged. "You know, we were sent down here by your boss." "You were?"

Jake picked up the bait. "Uh, yeah!" he said with a very unconvincing but enthusiastic nod. "Theresa told us specifically to come to you and, um, have a … chat?" Lily could see he was trying hard not to stare at the cage. Gwai growled. "You are lying."

Tara made a puzzled face. "He is?" The giant grinned proudly at them. "Oh, yes. My brain is special. It is made of clockwork!" "Literally?" Stacy asked. The golden giant nodded vigorously.

Suddenly Lily had an extremely stupid (emphasis on *stupid*) idea, as usual. She looked up at Gwai. "You know what? That's so impressive! But one thing that your clock brain can't detect is our plan!" she shouted. Lily pointed at Jake, Stacy, and Tara. "With a wave of my hand, I can, uh, take over these imbeciles' stupid minds!"

Okay, now she was starting to sound like Theresa herself. "You lie," Gwai said. "Suit yourself, I'll prove it!" Lily answered. She waved her hand dramatically at her friends. "You are now under my control," Lily said in a monotone. Tara and the others looked at her, confused. As Lily glared at them they followed her directions.

Stacy was the first to respond. She wailed and fell against Tara, who fell against Jake, and they all tumbled to the floor in a heap, rolling around and moaning comically. Up above, Gwai leaned down to take a closer look. "You see?" Lily yelled. "Beware my powers!"

Jake immediately stopped thrashing around and stared at Lily, like: *Are you kidding me?* Lily tried to ignore his stare and glared up at the giant's face. "Well?" she shouted. "What are you going to do, huh?" "You don't have to do anything," a voice laughed.

A wave of gray mist circled down from above and covered Jake. The misty horizontal cyclone spun fast, sending white things floating through the air. Lily caught one and realized it was a feather. The white downy fluff covered Tara and Stacy, who had sat up in amazement. Then the mist cleared. Standing in front of them was a white chicken. "Squawk?" The chicken looked down at his feathers. "*Jake?*" Stacy said. "SQUAWK!" Jake the chicken hopped around, waving his wings frantically. Stacy scooped him into her arms before Gwai stepped on him. "HA!" The giant roared with laughter. "The elf is a chicken! Ha!"

"Keep him distracted," Lily said to Tara. Tara yelled at the giant, "Hey! Theresa actually sent us to destroy you! She thinks you're the *ugliest creation in the world!*" "WHAT?" Gwai stepped towards them and Lily took her chance. She ran behind the giant's legs as he bent down, low enough for her to see the control panel on the back of his head. The metal ridges would have to do for a ladder. Lily kept her mind on clocks and got to work.

Tick, tock. Climb the ladder. *Tick, tock.* Done. Get up the back. Watch out! *Tick, tock.* Be careful of the arm. Hang on! *Tick, tock.* Halfway there. Uh oh, Tara's in trouble. *Tick tock.* The back's too hard to climb, use the arm. *Tick, tock.* Jump from the back to the arm. Mind the gap! *Tick, tock.* Get to the control panel.

Lily reached the back of Gwai's head and pried it open with her sword. The sheet of metal clanged to the floor fifteen feet below. In front of her was a giant clock crisscrossed with wires. Lily disconnected one from the clock and Gwai froze. Lily did some more adjustments, setting the clock so it rotated counter-clockwise and disconnecting and connecting random wires to each other, hoping she could get off the giant before he went BOOM. For good measure, she scratched up the clock's giant surface with her sword. She carefully climbed down the giant, dragging the power cord with her. She reached the ground. "Get somewhere safe," she said to the others. Lily patted the chicken on the head and went to a corner of the basement. “Do not fail me,” she said to the wires. Lily connected the power cord.

Gwai shuddered as Lily dropped the power cord and backed away. His body sparked and smoked, and with a massive groan, he began to fall apart as tiny fires erupted from between the metal plates covering him. He fell backward and his head slammed into the stone ceiling. The basement groaned and creaked as rubble rained down from the ceiling. Lily reached the cage and threw the cloth back. Her friends groaned. The cage was empty, a mere distraction from Theresa. Squawk the chicken (it was too strange to call him Jake, so they named him that) squawked and wriggled in Stacy’s arms. “Oh, shut up,” Stacy scolded crossly. The chicken continued to thrash, dropping out of Stacy’s arms with a light *thump*. He waddled behind the cage and pecked at a small hole, where a draft of air came out.

The wall slid back, revealing a small tunnel. They ran into it as Gwai fell flat on his face, Tara carrying Squawk in her arms.

Chapter 43

Tara vandalizes a tunnel

Being a chicken was extremely disturbing.

To be a small feathered bird was horrible. Jake couldn't do anything but squawk - and then to make things worse, his friends actually renamed him *Squawk*. I mean, seriously - what kind of name was that? Thanks a *lot*, Lily.

He looked towards the end of the tunnel as Tara used her sword to scratch the pure gold off the walls. Typical of Theresa to choose the most luxurious decorations for a tunnel. Jake felt himself sailing through the air as Tara tossed him to Stacy. To his surprise, Stacy set him down on the floor. "Just because I'm being nice," she said, "I'll let you walk by yourself." Jake adjusted to his role of Squawk the chicken and followed his friends.

***

Lily jogged to the end of the tunnel. There was a locked door in front of her. "Squawk," Jake/Squawk the chicken said. "Yeah, I know," Lily said bitterly. "Squawk!" Gray mist seeped under the door. It surrounded the chicken for five seconds, and then *bam* - Jake was sitting on the floor in front of them. He groaned and stood up. "Man, being a bird sucked." He glared at Lily. "And don't ever tempt Theresa like that. You know what she's like." "Uh ... sorry?" Lily used her sword to pry open the door.

Chapter 43: Tara vandalizes a tunnel

Theresa sat in her already-fixed throne, drinking a cup of coffee. She had turned an entire wall into a huge glass window, and Lily was pretty sure nothing would stop her from crashing through and escaping. Also, the gaping hole in the floor had been repaired. "Did you have a nice talk?" the queen asked. "Oh, yes, we did," Tara said sarcastically. "Oh, you're so happy," Theresa said, mocking Tara. "Hello, Jake. You make a very nice chicken, you know." "Theresa, where are our families?" Stacy asked. "Hmm?" the sorceress answered. "I turned them into mist. I'll be sending them off anytime now." "Wait, what?" Tara said.

Theresa threw her coffee cup over her shoulder at the window, making a hole in the glass and splashing liquid everywhere. Cold air rushed in. The queen waved her hand and a stream of gray mist flew through the hole and disappeared.

"Where did you take them?" Jake demanded. Theresa got up from her throne. "To my favorite vacation spot, of course. I've been there so many times." A gray video screen popped up, showing a woman and a younger version of Theresa arguing. Behind them, there was a city, packed with houses on a desert plain. The other lady was yelling, "Theresa! I *shall not* let you take over." Theresa screamed right back, "Thy brain must be scrambled. You clearly do not have my power, and if you do not let me rule, I shall destroy thy city." Gray fire lit up the houses, and the video vanished.

Due to Lily's history knowledge, Theresa had been speaking in the kind of language from somewhere in the time B.C or A.C. "Uh, you must have been really young," she said. In front of her, the sorceress raised her eyebrows. "There are many advantages of a magical life. But you do not know how long it took me to change to modern talk. Took me centuries, but now, I am more modern. Anyway, your families, like

I said, are in my favorite vacation spot." "Uh, can you give us, like, GPS or something?" Lily asked.

Theresa looked at her. "Actually, no, because I was planning to destroy all of you, which I shall do in about five seconds."

Chapter 44

Theresa takes a vacation

Lily pushed Stacy aside as Theresa sent a magical charge through the floor, making it cave in partway. She used her dagger to deflect flying debris and followed the others to the edge of the room. Jake jumped over a gap in the floor. “Goodbye!” Theresa said. “I’ll see you at the Empire State.” She turned into mist and zipped through the hole in the window.

The moment the queen left the window, the palace doors banged open. Pieces of the ceiling above fell and smashed holes in what was left of the floor. Lily realized that Theresa’s magic was the only thing keeping the prison from falling apart. “We need to get out of here!” she shouted. “I noticed!” Tara replied. They edged around the room and ran out the door as the palace fell completely, scattering dust with a massive BOOM. Foxfire came up with the other robot animals and Lily climbed on, riding away as chunks of rock burrowed into the ground.

They reached the elfin city in ten minutes. Lily slid off Foxfire’s back, patted him on the head, and led the way into the northern tower. A crowd of angry people was waiting for them. They pushed their way through the mob of crazy elves and went to a conference room, where they could talk in peace. Luckily, Jake found a way to get to that room secretly. Stacy ripped a map of the elfin world off the wall and spread it on the table. “Now, where could Theresa be?” she asked.

Lily glared at the map. "Not at her prison, that was destroyed." "And she wouldn't be in the elfin city, because that would be very annoying," Tara added.

Suddenly the map crackled, and a stream of mist erupted from Theresa's palace, weaving its way to the edge of the map, where it disappeared completely. Jake frowned. "That's impossible. We have charted our world entirely and accurately." "Unless Theresa's not on this planet ..." Stacy said. Lily looked around the room. Her heart began to pound as she tore a map of Earth off the wall. Immediately, the stream of gray mist appeared in the center of Alaska, leaping across the map until it reached a place Lily knew only too well.

Tara squinted at the map. "What in the elfin world? Where is that place?" she asked. Lily stared at the spot, labeled neatly with the three words that represented her home: NEW YORK CITY.

Chapter 44: Theresa takes a vacation

PART 3:

ON EARTH

Chapter 45

A three months wait

It took three months to rebuild the P.O.O.P. and the rest of the elfin city, which meant three months of planning, convincing the other elves that Lily wasn't the enemy, and making up dangerous recipes for dangerous weapons. Now Lily sat at a table, surrounded by her friends Stacy, Tara, and Jake.

"Unbelievable," Jake said. He used his new sword to stab the map sitting on the table. "Why would Theresa choose New York?" "Because it's so far away," Tara answered. Stacy chimed in, "AND it's on Earth." Lily sighed. "Guys, less arguing and more thinking, okay? The P.O.O.P. is going to be ready any minute."

"Oh, fine," Tara said. Jake pointed at the map of New York. "I think that Theresa would be next to the Empire State Building." "No, the New York Stock Exchange Building," Stacy said. "No, the Statue of Liberty." "No, 56th Street." "No, the-"

"Hey!" Lily shouted. "You're arguing again!" "Guys, what's that sound?" Tara asked.

Footsteps clattered down the hallway and an elf poked her head inside the room. "We're all ready for transport," she said.

Jake grabbed his sword from the map. "Let's go, hurry up," he said. They followed the elf back up the hallway, where a brand new, shiny and ready to use P.O.O.P. was waiting for them. Another elf was standing next to the transport machine. "Do you have your weapons?" he asked. Everyone nodded. "Dart guns?" "Yes." "Swords?" "Yes." "Gas bombs?"

Silence. Tara sighed. "Jake, you idiot; I told you to get the bomb bags."

Jake held up his hands in exasperation. "How can you expect me to collect all the weapons for all of you when I'm dealing with problems of my own?" At that moment, an elf ran up, holding the bomb bags. They each took one and clipped it to their belt. Another elf pressed a button and the weapons turned invisible. "I guess we're ready to go," Lily said.

They went over to the transport container. "I forgot to tell you," Stacy whispered to Lily, "once we arrive, we'll be next to the Empire State Building, but you'll be back in school, same as before you left." "Thanks for the warning," Lily said. They squeezed into the box and the cover slid over.

Two minutes later the box stopped. Lily was at first alarmed because she actually *felt* the box stop, but then everyone (including the box) vanished and Lily was sitting at her school desk. Ms. Anne was still at her desk, saying, "Get on to your textbook app. Jimmy, don't jump on your seat." Lily found she was still holding her iPad, and the password she had typed in - Schoolgirl72 - had worked. She went to her iBooks app and started reading as her teacher began the social studies lesson.

Chapter 46

The new girl in school

After school, Lily grabbed her backpack and took the bus home. She went up the stairs in her apartment building to the 3rd floor and went inside her room. Her mother greeted her with a hug. "How was school?" she asked. "It was fine, mom," Lily replied. For a second, she was tempted to say, *oh, I was abducted by some elves, but I'm fine now. I was in a war, mom!*

"Your father and brother are still in Canada." Lily's mother said. Of *course*, Dad was still on his work trip, and Peter was still with him. "Yup." "Oh, and you just missed the visitor." Lily's stomach lurched. "Visitor?" "Mmm-hmm. Young woman wearing a simple purple dress. Is she a friend of yours?" Lily tried not to throw up. "Uh, yes," she answered. "Her name's Theresa. You know what? I'm going to take a walk. See you soon, mom." Lily walked out of her room and started down the stairs.

On the second floor stairs, a voice sounded behind her: "Dear, can you help me?" An old woman stood halfway down the stairs, holding out her hand. "Sure," Lily smiled. She extended her hand and the woman grabbed it.

The old lady's grip was like iron. Lily tried to shake her hand free without success. "Hey!" she said. "Let me go!" The woman straightened up, becoming younger, her clothes turning into a simple purple dress. "Hello, Lily," Theresa said.

Chapter 46: The new girl in school

"What are you doing here?" Lily demanded. The sorceress queen smiled. "I am only here for a warning," she said. "What?" Lily asked. Theresa whispered in her ear, "Watch for the others. My sister can be quite dangerous when she wants to." Lily knew instantly she was talking about Tara's and the other's families. But when did Theresa have a sister? The queen vanished into gray mist.

"Well, you came back quickly," Lily's mother said. "I was feeling tired, so, um, I'll just stay home," Lily answered.

It was hard sleeping that night because Lily was sure that Theresa would come back for her. But eventually, sleep took over, and she closed her eyes.

The next morning Lily was working on her math morning work in school when her teacher suddenly said, "Okay, class, say hello to our newest student. Since these are the last five days of school before summer vacation, she's only visiting, and then she'll join the school like everyone else." At that moment, the classroom door opened and a girl came in. Lily had never seen her more serious before.

"Why don't you introduce yourself?" Ms. Anne said. "My name is Oneida. I am from California," Oneida said. "Well, thank you," Lily's teacher said. "There's an empty seat next to Lily, you can sit there. Lily, Oneida, try to get to know each other." Oneida walked stiffly to her desk and sat down.

During lunch, Lily and Oneida sat at an empty table. Somehow, Oneida had a ham sandwich with her. As they were eating, she said, "I was not truthful." "You did fine," Lily assured. "No." Oneida turned to face Lily. "I am not from California. I am from the elfin world. I do not know how I really got here, but I know Theresa was part of it. My family is very far away from here. How could I be truthful if I didn't say all this?" "Jake's at the Empire State Building. Also, you could be more cheerful than this." "You'd be sorry if I was complaining to you 24/7." The school bell rang and they returned to their homeroom. As they walked up the stairs, Oneida whispered, "I'll be more cheerful if I live through geography class."

After school, Lily introduced Oneida to her mother, saying that she would be staying for a while. "Her parents are working in England," she explained. Lily's mom gave Oneida the guest room and said she would let her stay for the weekend.

When Lily's mom had gone to sleep, Lily went to Oneida's temporary room. "Be careful," she said. "Theresa told me to watch out for her sister." Oneida's face went pale. "There could only be one reason why Sophie is on Earth. She wants revenge on Theresa." "For what?" Lily asked. "Sophie locked her own sister in that prison, to keep her from destroying her ever-growing city. Now that Theresa has broken free, she wants to track her down and capture her again." Lily thought for a moment. "But how can I tell who she is?" she pressed. "Her magic is gray, like Theresa's," Oneida said. "She is the most powerful in her family, more powerful than Theresa. Sophie will stop at nothing to capture Theresa, but she will want you as a prize if she is in a good mood."

Chapter 47

Sophie arrives (and the Statue of Liberty comes to life)

Lily and Oneida took the bus to the Empire State Building. As soon as Oneida spotted Jake, she became much more cheerful ("Jake, where have you been? I have to go to school now, and geography class is horrible ...")

Afterward, they all went to the Statue of Liberty, where they could talk and enjoy the view at the same time. "Theresa's sister is coming," Lily said. Stacy groaned. "Oh, not her again." "She destroyed nearly half of the elfin city ten years ago and exploded the candy store," Tara explained. "Worst day of my life," Stacy said. "Can we stop talking and actually go to the statue?" Jake asked. In front of them, the Statue of Liberty stood, tall and proud with a torch in hand.

"We could take a cruise ship," Stacy offered. "But the lines are too long," Lily said. The two admission lines were filled with at least fifty people each. Strangely, the huge boats were empty. But to her right, Lily saw a duck, floundering near the boats. The workers were trying to get it out of the water. But for a second, its form flickered, turning gray and transparent.

Lily nudged Stacy. "Are you seeing this?" she asked. "Yeah," Stacy whispered back. Jake frowned. "If the duck isn't real, it should be gray, the work of Theresa." "But Sophie's also on Earth," Tara said. "And Sophie's magic is gray ..." Oneida stared at the duck.

Besides them, the people waiting in line seemed to take no notice. Lily realized that the duck only turned gray when it looked at them, and the duck never looked at the people. Whenever a worker got too close for comfort, it swam further away, quacking in defiance. Suddenly it disappeared underwater. "Sophie should be here somewhere," Stacy said. Oneida squinted at the water. "The duck's disappeared," she said. Lily looked up. "Guys, maybe we should leave," she warned. "We're not safe here ..." "But where's Sophie?" Jake asked.

A flash of black caught her eye. It came from the observation deck of the Statue of Liberty. Someone, a woman, was standing there. Even from fifty feet away, Lily could see how she possessed Theresa's smile. She vanished in a flash of gray.

"Tara," Lily warned, "get Oneida and go somewhere safe. Jake, you, too." "Why?" Tara asked. Five seconds later, the statue rumbled. "She's in the statue!" Lily screamed. A massive shockwave of gray light expanded outwards from the statue, sending everyone sprawling in a high-speed spray of water. The statue shuddered and came to life, snarling. Its eyes locked on Lily. With a disdainful look, it vanished, leaving behind several curls of gray mist.

Lily groaned and sat up. Her friends lay sodden on the grass. Already, the wailing of police sirens and ambulances could be heard. As Lily struggled to stand up a force slammed into her, knocking her flat on her back.

Chapter 47: Sophie arrives (and the Statue of Liberty comes to life)

A young woman over her. Her long, straight hair was a blonde color that could have been mistaken for white. She was dressed in a black motorcycle jacket and pants.

"Where is my sister?" she said. "You mean Theresa?" Lily asked. Sophie's eyes blazed as she sent gray mist curling around Lily's arms, lifting her to her feet. "Yes, Theresa," she said. Lily sighed, trying not to show the mixed emotions stirring inside of her. "Well, you've come to the wrong place, because she isn't here."

"I know who you are, Lilith Claire," Sophie said. The gray magic tightened around Lily's arms, making her wince. "First, I would prefer to be called *Lily*. And I don't know where Theresa is," Lily protested. "Obviously, you know," Theresa's sister hissed. "Scaredy-cat."

As the sorceress raised her hand to strike, she suddenly flew backward. Lily gasped for air (Sophie had apparently been strangling her with mist - pretty stupid, right?) as she fell onto the ground. Sophie got to her feet and almost immediately fell to her knees, clutching at her head. In a swirl of gray mist, an all-too-familiar figure wearing a purple dress appeared behind her. "Hello, sister," Theresa said.

"It's been a long time since you called me 'sister,' Theresa," Sophie said. Theresa sighed in exasperation. "You imprisoned me in that palace 50 years ago, Sophie. You have never visited me since." The queen sent gray mist flying towards her sister, but Sophie was faster. She thrust out her hand and the mist flipped direction, spiraling backward and curling around Theresa. "I could capture you right at this moment," Sophie mused. "You were foolish to come here, *sister*." "Ha! I have become much more powerful over the past few years," Theresa replied.

Lily, who had been sitting on the ground, staring at the two in amazement, snapped back to her senses as she heard a groan behind her. Tara sat up, rubbing her head. "Lily, what just happened? I feel so-gah!" Tara scrambled backward in the grass on her hands and feet. She pulled a grenade out of her pocket as she looked at Theresa in shock. "Go away, Theresa! I promise I'll throw this at you!" she yelled. Theresa rolled her eyes. "Nice to see you too, Tara."

Sophie suddenly attacked Theresa again, lifting her off her feet. The queen thrashed and kicked as gray mist curled around her arms. Theresa's sister looked at Lily one more time. "Stay away from my sister," she hissed. "If you dare seek me, remember the Statue of Liberty, and just think about what I can do." With a flash of gray, they both disappeared, leaving two objects glimmering in the grass.

Lily peered into the grass and picked up an emerald and a sapphire. Oneida, who had just regained consciousness, stared at the sparkling jewels. "Sophie's and Theresa's symbols of power," she said. "Stay away. They might be dangerous." They helped Jake and Stacy to their feet and staggered away from the scene. But Lily did notice something about the gemstones. In the heart of the sapphire, there was a small spot of gray that was sparking and spreading throughout the gem, slowly consuming it and turning it into an emerald, which could only mean one thing. Sophie was much more powerful than they thought. Little by little, she was poisoning her sister's magic and energy.

Chapter 48

A text on the phone

Lily led the others to her apartment home. Her mother didn't even blink as they passed by her, into Lily's room. As soon as Oneida shut the door Jake pulled a tiny cannon out of his pocket. "If Theresa's gone wild with her sister, there's only one solution," he said. He handed the cannon to Lily. "Fire the tracker out the window." Lily yanked open her bedroom window and fired a small sphere outside. Instantly, it sparked and dissolved into dust that blew away in the wind.

"Okay ... apparently Theresa knows our location," Jake muttered. "She's been here before," Lily replied.

Ding! Ding! Everyone froze and looked at Lily's bed. Lily walked over and pulled her phone out from under her pillow. "Someone sent me a text," she said. She opened her phone and frowned. "Guys, take a look at this." The text (actually, there were two texts) read:

August 4th, 2037

Ugh! Lily, I am bored! Hurry up! I am WAITING.

#TheresatheQueen

August 10th, 2037

Sophie is after me and I am not running away. That is how BORED I am! So HURRY UP!

#TheresatheQueen

"What in the world? When did Theresa get a phone?" Stacy demanded. "She doesn't need a phone," Tara answered. Lily threw her iPhone back on her bed in disgust. "Guys, whatever. Let's get on with this." She dug a map of New York City out of her nearby backpack (a souvenir from geography class) and spread it on her desk, sliding a small bucket of paper pins towards her. "So, what do we know?" Oneida reached over and stabbed a pin into the Statue of Liberty. "We know that the Statue of Liberty came to life and vanished afterward. That was where we first saw Sophie."

Lily nodded. "Very good." "But we need more information," Jake said. "Where will Sophie strike next?"

They spent the next half hour decorating the map with pins, color coded for possible targets. Finally, they speculated that Sophie and her sister were most likely to strike at the Empire State Building, the NYSE building or Central Park.

Lily stepped back and pointed at the Empire State Building on the map. "Sophie will most likely attack there. I'm sure of it." "I don't know," Jake said. "I mean, she could be anywhere. For Sophie and Theresa, transportation isn't a problem."

Chapter 48: A text on the phone

Tara kicked the table. "We should stop them from transporting. I say we launch an attack." "But what about our families? I think we should find the others, and *then* attack," Stacy protested.

"Lily! It's dinnertime! Come on down," Lily's mother shouted. Lily sighed and carefully put the map on top of her dresser. "We'll work on this later. Let's go." Five minutes later, Lily watched her friends board a bus and drive away. Oneida, who was going to stay for another night, squeezed Lily's hand. "We still have hope. Theresa can't have a plan already." "She doesn't," Lily replied. "We all know that Sophie is chasing her, trying to capture her sister and imprison her again. When I looked into that sapphire in the grass, its center was gray. You were right, Oneida. Sophie is more powerful than Theresa. But not in the way you would have imagined. Sophie is sapping Theresa's magic."

Oneida paced back and forth. "Lily, do you recall how strong Theresa's powers were in the elfin world? And now she's so weak on Earth." "So you're saying that Theresa was so used to the elfin world that she's actually weaker on this planet?" Oneida nodded. "Fifty years in prison can do that to a person."

"Dinnertime!" Lily's mother shouted from the kitchen. "I'm coming, Mom!" Lily yelled. "I hope that my mom didn't turn dinner to charcoal. She's that bad at cooking." Oneida smirked.

Turns out, dinner was *not* charcoal, but it was pretty close. Lily crunched her way through the last of her plate of blackened chicken and brushed her teeth. She headed to bed without further conversation. As she lay down, she thought of Sophie chasing them and shuddered.

Chapter 49

A reunion at Kmart

The next morning Lily and her friends gathered near Central Park. Stacy gave a brief report. "I saw Theresa last night from my hotel window. I'm sure it was her. She was walking, possibly running, in the direction of the Statue of Liberty's location - at least, until it disappeared." "Which is away from here," Tara said. "We can still try to blend in. I already have ideas." She pointed to all of them, one by one. "Lily and Oneida, you should be fine. Stay in school as long as you can. Stacy, I'm thinking you should be, um, a volunteer for Lily's school. I'll think about what I can do. But Jake ..." Tara thought for a moment. "You need a job."

Jake looked incredulous. "Who, me?" "Yeah. There's an opening for cashiers at the Kmart over there," Tara replied distractedly. "But-"

"I'm starving!" Stacy announced. Food must've been on everyone's mind because Lily and her friends began to search for a restaurant. "There's a McDonald's over there." Lily pointed.

"No, there isn't."

"Jake, I'm sure. See the big M?"

"Stacy, do you see it?"

"Uh, wait ... Tara, I see it!"

"I see it too!"

"Me too! I am *starving*!"

They reached the McDonald's and went in, ordering a jumbo fries and hamburgers and an extra-large salad (Tara was a vegetarian.) In a few minutes, Lily and the others were inhaling fries. Tara munched down her salad. Soon, full of fast food, they went to the Kmart to see if they could get anything of actual value.

As they got closer to the store, Lily heard a shuffling sound. Jake yelped in surprise as he was dragged into a nearby alley by someone in a black sweatshirt. After a few moments of shouting, Jake and the stranger began to talk. Lily stopped the others from running into the alley as Jake began to speak:

"Gah! Whaa..."

"Yo, little dude."

"Parker, I am *very* glad to see you, but for the last time, I am *not* little! Why are you wearing that?"

"Thank you for noticing. How many times have you hit your head?"

"Okay, just because I hit my head a billion times back home doesn't mean I have to hit my head on Earth."

"Yeah. It's been, like, several hours since I've eaten, and you smell like fast food. Do you have a hamburger?"

"Actually, no."

There were more scuffling sounds and soon Parker came out of the alley, dragging Jake like a naughty dog. Oneida instantly pounced on him, scolding, "Parker, where have you been? You idiot - that is no way to treat your poor little sister, by which I mean *me*, leaving her all alone ..." and so on. Jake snuck off back to the McDonald's and bought his older brother a hamburger. Parker munched on it and stood politely, watching as Oneida rambled on and on for what seemed like hours on end. Eventually, she ran out of breath. Parker finished off his burger and smacked Jake on the back, nearly knocking him over. "Well, bro, we better get going. I hear Theresa's been up to naughty stuff! Messing up the Statue of Liberty, what an accomplishment!"

Lily decided to interrupt the conversation before Jake started screaming. "That wasn't Theresa, that was Sophie," she said. The color drained from Parker's face. "Say what?" "Theresa is being chased by her sister," Stacy explained. "She's even more powerful than we thought," Oneida added. "Gradually, she's sapping Theresa's energy and her powers."

Parker took a deep breath. "Well, I wasn't expecting that. She devastated the elfin city ten years ago; back in, uh, 2027. Sophie destroyed half of the city. I wasn't hurt, but I got pretty freaked out when she left Jake dangling from the twentieth floor outside the damaged main center." "I was only 147 years old," Jake complained. "I don't know. I would be so sad if she demolished all the candy stores on this planet," Parker said with a shake of his head. Next to Lily, Stacy shuddered, as if recalling the terrible candy incident. "Anyway, Theresa dropped us all over New York City. I fell in a trash can. Ouch."

"We can all be sympathetic and cry later, but we need to find my mom and Stacy's sister," Tara interrupted. "Right!" Jake smacked

Parker's back, who turned around and hit Jake on his back, sending him sprawling. "Ow." Stacy helped Jake to his feet and they all began towards the Empire State Building after Lily suggested it.

As they were walking down 5th street Stacy suddenly stopped in her tracks and whispered, "Do you hear that?" Coming from their right side was the sound of a toddler screaming and crying. "*Stacy*!" Stacy dashed into the street and disappeared around the block, coming back seconds later with her sister Sandra in her arms. Sandra had stopped crying and was now focused on eating the end of her flowered shirt. "I found her next to a garbage can," she said happily. They took a detour and dropped off Sandra at Lily's home before continuing their walk.

Chapter 50

Sophie makes an appearance

When they reached the Empire State Building, they were immediately met by a strange sight. Police cars surrounded the humongous skyscraper. When Lily requested access inside, the officers all said NO. Eventually, Lily decided to take a risk and asked the captain himself, who said, "We can't risk another landmark being destroyed. Anyway, I'll be fired if the Empire State Building turns into a freaking monster." Lily took their response as a longer version of NO. Frustrated, Lily led the others behind a dumpster nearby. "I am going to get in that building," she whispered. "Lily, you must be crazy. Can't you see the police?" Tara replied. Truth be told, Lily wasn't sure why she wanted to get inside, but she decided not to argue any longer. She grabbed a grenade from her bag and pressing the detonation button, she kicked it up. It sailed into the air with a massive BOOM.

Police officers whipped around with shouts of surprise. Lily took her chance and led her friends inside the Empire State Building unnoticed.

Lily had been inside the skyscraper many times. However, she was stunned by the building's emptiness. There were no lights, and Lily got confused as she rummaged through her bomb bag until Parker handed her a small flashlight. When Lily clicked it on, it expanded into a full size glowing gray transparent shield. It reminded her too much of

Theresa, but she kept it anyway. Brandishing the shield, she crept up a flight of stairs, closely followed by her friends.

Soon they reached a door that said, KEEP OUT. Lily pointed at the sign. "Is that me, or does that sound like Theresa would be in there?" Nobody answered. "Just stay here. I'm going in."

Lily opened the door and walked through. Unsurprisingly, the room was empty. A small lamp shone dimly. Cautious, Lily turned off the shield and was sliding it into her pocket when someone caught her from behind.

"Crap!" Lily struggled to escape, her arm in the grasp of a stranger. The woman hissed in her ear. "Hello, Lily. Where is my sister?" Now Lily knew who she was talking to. "Sophie, for the hundredth time, I *don't* know." Sophie sighed. "Pity."

Gray mist surrounded Lily's head. She could feel Theresa's sister forcing her way into her mind, trying to take over. "Get out of my head!" she said. She kicked backward with one foot and Sophie stumbled away.

Lily staggered to the wall, fumbling a bomb from her weapons bag. As Sophie approached she spiked it as far away as possible from her, knocking the sorceress off her feet. Sophie struck at Lily, sending her tumbling over the floor. Lily got to her feet and backed against the wall. In front of her, Theresa's sister snarled. Her white hair was tangled from the fight. As Sophie thrust out her hand, someone came out of nowhere and tackled her.

"Ack!" Sophie fell over, arms flailing. Oneida stood a small distance away from Lily, her eyes filled with fear and uncertainty. Lily could tell what she was thinking: *Should I run?* "You *miserable* girl," Sophie muttered. She sent a gray missile flying at Oneida, who pressed herself against the far wall, shaking.

It was now or never. Lily jumped over the missile, grabbing her flashlight. She ran for Oneida and slammed the activation button with her thumb on the flashlight. Instantly, it expanded into a shield - and only just in time! The mist missile detonated against the gray dome. Sparks flew by the millions.

Apparently, the shield couldn't stand the sparks any longer, because it actually lost some of its color and cracked. Sophie growled and sent an entire wall of gray mist sailing toward both of them. Oneida covered her nose immediately and Lily used her cracked shield to protect her face. Over the commotion, Sophie said, "Oh, one more thing. If you're looking for Theresa, you'll easily know where she is if she hasn't fled from this planet already."

Sophie disappeared in a flash of mist just as Lily chucked her shield at the sorceress. *BLONG!* It smashed against the wall and shattered into a million pieces. The door to the room crashed open. Jake and Parker rushed inside. "Oneida!" Jake rushed forward and gave his little sister a big hug. "All right, go away," Oneida grumbled, "before I ask Parker to smack you." "Oh, come on!" Parker held up what was left of his flashlight shield. "This cost me a ton of money!" he said, tossing it back at her. "I'm sorry," Lily said innocently. While Parker's back was turned, she stuck out her tongue at him.

Chapter 51

A robot dinosaur gets wrecked

As soon as Lily and Oneida exited the room, Tara and Stacy pounced on them, demanding they tell what happened and saying that they wouldn't leave the building unless Lily explained NOW. When they were finally satisfied, Jake shut the door and they started the long task of getting out of the Empire State Building without being noticed. The police officers were still positioned around the skyscraper, so Lily eventually had to dig out another grenade from her bag and blow up the nearest tree as a distraction.

Afterward, things got easy. Lily caught up with a hoverbus (things have changed for the vehicles of 2037) and after a few seconds, told the driver to follow a gray trail of mist leading to Theresa's hiding place. When she and her friends arrived at the house, it was around 5:00 in the afternoon. They paid the bus driver and climbed out of the bus. As they walked down the sidewalk, Lily heard Stacy say, "Look at all the robots."

Lily peered into the street, looking at the robot animals: the greatest creatures to arrive in electronics. There was a dog, a cat, and a bird, all going around randomly on the sidewalk. Jake blinked. "I heard that there was a fourth robot. Scientists wanted it to be the biggest and the strongest of its kind. They didn't even bother trying to make it resemble any normal animal. In fact, it was meant to be a secret to the people of Earth. But it turned wild and disappeared."

Tara glanced down the street. "Well, it isn't here. See, look: there are only three robots." CRUNCH. Lily froze. Slowly, she turned around.

It took Lily a while to take in the massive metal form looming in front of her, munching down on a lamppost. The robot seemed vaguely familiar, with a name that Lily couldn't quite place. Her friends had turned around, gaping at the thing looking down at them. "Nobody ... moves ... a...muscle," Lily whispered through gritted teeth. Tara stepped backward and bumped into a wall.

ROAR! The robot leaped at them. Its teeth and eyes flashed with a petrifying menace. Now, Lily realized the kind of robot the scientists had cooked up in their lab: a Tyrannosaurus Rex. "Go, go, go!" Lily grabbed Oneida's hand and they sprinted out of the street. Oneida was faster that her, and soon her hand slipped from Lily's grasp. The others ran past her, ducking for cover as the humongous T. Rex emerged from the street, demolishing buildings like they were made from paper and bellowing in rage. Lily was so overcome with fear she felt glued to the ground. She knew she should run, but something kept her back. She and her friends needed a place to hide. Lily wasn't sure if the strongest bomb shelter in the world would stand the weight of a ten-ton dinosaur.

Already, the wailing of police sirens was echoing around them. "Lily, what are you doing?" Tara yelled. Lily snapped back to her senses and dashed after the others, pursued by the metal monster. She managed to catch up with Parker. "We need weapons!" he said. *Weapons* ... where could they find weapons? Lily patted her pockets, only to find that she and her friends' bomb bags had flown away from them, rolling towards the apparently magnetic robot. The dinosaur was completely blocking the police department. Stacy grabbed her arm, preventing her from crashing into a wall. A big window revealed people walking around with luggage bags. The place had to be an airport ... considerably big enough to hide. Lily found the door and burst through, slamming it shut once her friends joined her. They ran through the crowd and dove into the nearest Radio Shack store.

Lily ran through a list of the most deadly things possible that you could make out of a phone. A blinding camera flash? Deafening music? No such luck. But there weren't just phones. Lily started towards the chainsaw aisle and almost immediately tripped over a box of heat-seeking tracker missiles. How *that* ended up in this shop, Lily would never know. She decided it was good for starters. She marched up to the register. The cashier looked up. "Oh, that? Uh, fifty dollars and forty-seven cents, please."

Lily patted her empty pockets in frustration. Her hand bumped into the remains of the gray shield. She grabbed it and waved it in the man's face. "This is, uh, 100% authentic vintage *Star Wars* weaponry. If I were you, man, I would get it before the long lines for this thing start appearing."

Thirty seconds later, Lily lugged a large box of missiles out of the shop. She hid behind a big sign and emptied its contents. She quickly assembled them. Stacy gave advice whenever she got stuck. Lily loaded the first missile into the launcher as the front wall of the airport caved in, narrowly missing screaming travelers.

The robot dinosaur stepped through the rubble, and Lily fired the hopefully trustworthy heat-seeking missile. With a high-pitched *whee*, the missile sailed into the robot's *gluteus maximus* and detonated. The dinosaur crumbled apart into a pile of smoking metal. Tara led the others towards it.

Stacy kicked the steaming pile of metal. "This," she declared, "will make a strange news story."

Chapter 52

Theresa again

Lily caught up with yet another hoverbus and dropped Oneida and Parker at the hotel before going back to Theresa's hideout. She stomped to the door and banged on it. She and the others waited on the porch, until the door finally swung open, revealing Theresa. She glared at them, her once beautiful face pale and weary. She looked over at the six people standing in front of her. "This better be good." Theresa stepped aside, revealing a dark and tidy house. "Come in."

Everyone ended up seated in front of a television. The screen showed the news: buildings demolished, an airport badly damaged, reports of a robot dinosaur melting into a smoking piece of metal after being hit by a missile. Funny how fast news can spread. "Why did you come?" Theresa asked. Jake sat forward. "We would like to discuss something with you," he said. He shut off the television. "Your sister. Where is she?"

Theresa sighed. "I wish I knew, but sadly, I don't." She wrung her hands. "Sophie had my location in less than a day. She left me in this house, stole my magic ... but I have hope." Theresa held up a small sapphire. "This is my backup. Only for emergencies." Lily noticed that her voice held no humor. She realized that Theresa's magic was the only thing that made her happy.

"But we *are* going to find Sophie," Stacy said reassuringly. Theresa stared at her until Stacy squirmed. "A foolish idea - a very dangerous mission. I will take my backup and go myself after you leave. The sapphire can be quite explosive when opened." "Theresa, you know it isn't safe," Lily said. Theresa looked at her. "I know, Lily. But it isn't safe for you, either. Your friends can't stay on this planet for long. Sophie would find them in a heartbeat if she wanted to. They aren't human." "So you mean ..." Lily's worst fears were confirmed as Tara nodded. "Lily, we have to go back without you, before Sophie finds us. We'll leave around the coming spring the latest. It's the best for everyone's safety. We need to stick to our plan." "What - so you were planning to leave all along?" Lily demanded. "It's not like that. We didn't know Sophie was here until the last second. We had to improvise ..."

Suddenly the house rumbled, and Theresa whipped around. "Sophie is here," she said. The doorbell rang a pleasant *ding*. Everyone froze, staring at the door. Was Sophie staying outside on purpose, taunting them to come out into the open? The doorbell rang, louder. When the knocking began, Theresa slowly approached the window and peeked out. The next thing Lily knew, the sorceress was coming at her, pushing her and the others back, away from the door. "What? What's going on?" Lily asked. "Stay down," Theresa muttered, "she's going to break in."

But Sophie didn't break in. At least, not through the door. What really happened was as the knocking on the door stopped, the house gave a tremendous shake and groan. Plaster from the ceiling rained down like paper. The floor and walls cracked. "Go! Get out!" Theresa screamed. Jake and the others stood, frozen in shock, as the roof partially caved in. "GO!" Lily yelled. Tara was the first to respond. She gave Jake a hard shove, and he stumbled forward, ducking to avoid falling debris. Still in the collapsing room, Lily saw Theresa leaning against the sofa, cupping the sapphire in her hands and murmuring something under her breath. What had she said only five minutes earlier? *The sapphire can be quite explosive when opened.* If that meant what Lily was thinking, the results wouldn't be good. "Darn, now we have to run," she whispered.

Lily grabbed Stacy's hand and sprinted after her friends into the kitchen. "Keep running and don't stop!" she shouted. "What's happening?" Stacy said. "Why are we running away from Sophie? We should be fighting her." But it wasn't Sophie Lily was worried about.

A loud BOOM shook the house. Glancing over her shoulder, Lily saw a shockwave of gray racing towards them, breaking walls apart like tissue paper. "Crap. Just go! Go!" she replied. She and Stacy managed to catch up with Jake and Tara. "Listen up. In a while, we're going to reach a certain destination. When I say jump, jump," Lily said to everyone. "Can't we duck?" Jake asked. "Shockwave's too big. But I know just the place," she answered. They scrambled over a hole in the wall as the house fell apart. Lily and her friends ran down the street. Now that the shockwave was outside, it expanded into a fifty-yard line of glowing destruction. "Lily, we're going nowhere!" Tara yelled. Lily was too out of breath to answer.

They crossed the road and staggered to a stop at the town park. Luckily, the weather was absolutely dreadful, so there would be no pedestrians having hallucinations of five people running away from mass destruction. "Hold your breath. When I count to three, run for the lake and jump," Lily told the others. "Lily, are you crazy?" Stacy asked. *Probably*, Lily thought. But all she said was, "I'm sure."

Suddenly, the miserable weather got worse. Dark clouds hovered overhead, and a loud clap of thunder momentarily distracted Lily. She looked up for five seconds at the dark clouds. "Lily! Do we jump?" Stacy said. Lily looked back and swore. The wave of gray was almost on them. She needed to give the signal. No time for a countdown.

"Three!" Lily yelled. She and her friends turned around and went for the lake. As the gray shockwave pressed against Lily's back, she held her breath and jumped into the town lake. The gray light careened over the surface of the water, slicing reeds like tissue paper, and stayed there.

Lily sank deeper and deeper into the water. She had lost her grasp on Stacy's hand in the darkness and confusion. Lily watched the glowing gray haze of Theresa's magic ripple back and forth until it finally disappeared. Lily swam for the surface as fast as she could. She needed air badly. She kicked upward and managed to reach the surface, gasping for oxygen and staring at the path of destruction Theresa's power left behind. Next to her, someone was floundering in the water - Jake, trying to say something. "Lily! *Glub.* What-*glub*-were you-*glub*-thinking? *Glub*-gah!-*glub*." "What?" Lily yelled. Tara and Stacy surfaced, Lily and Jake helping them to shore. Stacy coughed and shuddered. "I *hate* water!" "Then we get away from the water," Lily proposed. They staggered away from the lake.

The storm clouds cleared away in seconds. The police arrived within five minutes, and Lily and the others reached a McDonald's when their clothes finally dried out. Sure, they were still beaten up and miserable as can be, but at least they didn't look like they had blown up several streets while jumping in the lake, which would make everyone think of them as wet hooligans. They ate lunch sitting at a table in the corner.

Chapter 52: Theresa again

Lily wanted to go home, but she couldn't risk leading Sophie to her apartment. She went to the restaurant phone and called her mother. "Hey, mom." "How are you doing?" "I'm fine. Did Dad come back yet?" "No. By the way, Lily, I just got a call from my work manager. I'm going to Seattle for a work trip tomorrow, and I won't be back until Friday. Can you manage by yourself for two days?" "Yeah, thanks. See you later." Lily hung up the phone.

At 9:00 PM, Lily and her friends took a hoverbus to the nearest hotel. The sign that hung over the front door read: **THE VANILLA INN**. When they walked through the door, Lily smelled the faint scent of vanilla in the air. At the service counter, there was a young woman. "Would you like the luxury rooms or the ultimate luxury rooms?" she said sweetly. "We would like ..." Jake said. "Four luxury rooms, please," Lily said quickly. The woman typed something on a computer. "All right. $250," she said. Lily dug around in her pockets until she found her credit card. She scanned it and soon she was standing in a huge hotel room with a posh bedroom and a whole wall in the living room devoted to a panoramic glass window overlooking the whole of New York. No doubt Tara and the others had gotten the same quality. *If this is the luxury room, what will the ultimate luxury rooms be like?* Lily wondered.

She gathered everyone into her living room for a pep talk. "So," she prompted. "If we want to find Sophie before she blows up this planet, what should we do?"

For a few seconds, they fidgeted and looked at each other, like *dude, I don't have anything. Ideas?*

"Uh … flip a coin? Heads plan and tails find Sophie?" Lily suggested. "Heads," said Tara and Stacy. "Okay … I guess I'll take, uh, tails," Jake muttered.

"Wonderful," Lily said. "Now all we need is a coin." "Oh, I have one!" Jake fished a coin out of his pocket and it fell on the floor.

Ever heard of those expand-in-water sponge toys? That honest-to-goodness penny suddenly grew in size greatly, and when it was done, it wasn't just a giant heap of copper.

Somehow the penny had converted its shape and size into a full-size cannon, though its barrel was slightly larger. Tara stared at it. "That penny is *disturbing*," she announced. Jake peered into the barrel. "That ain't any cannon," he said. "It catapults artificial intelligence 'humans.'"

Lily stared at the fuse. "So that thing is an AI cannon. Well, we could have used that sooner." "Hey," Jake protested, "I didn't even know that thing was in my pocket! We have a bunch of these back in the elfin world. I must have grabbed one and put it in my jacket." "And then you forgot about it?" Stacy asked. "No, I didn't … yeah, I forgot."

While they talked, Tara had been walking around the cannon. She kicked the stand. Lily saw her. "Wait, Tara, don't-" she started to say.

And just as quickly as it appeared, the cannon shrunk back into a tiny penny. Jake scooped it off the floor and put it into his pocket.

"Okay, then," Lily said. "Meeting's done."

Chapter 53

Lily and her friends escape from a giant pigeon

The next morning the phone rang quite loudly. Lily woke with a yell of surprise and snatched up the phone. “Who is it?” she demanded.

“Lily?” a voice on the other end said.

“Theresa, what do you want?” Lily glanced at the clock, which told her it was 8:00 in the morning. “I sent Sandra and Marissa back to the elfin world. Jake’s siblings can still assist Jake in fighting Sophie, unless they really want to come back.” With that, Theresa hung up

Lily told a relieved Tara and Stacy their families were safe, thanks to Theresa. Stacy was still on alert, though. “We’re not safe,” she insisted. “Sophie might already be on her way as we speak.”

“We can get to Sophie first,” Lily assured. “We can *end* this battle once and for all.” And she kept her promise ... at least, the first part (sort of). That afternoon, they visited her apartment, where she grabbed her phone from her room and borrowed her mom’s car, giving Tara the keys in the hope that she wouldn’t crash the vehicle into a tree. After texting Theresa via #TheresatheQueen, she found out that Sophie was possibly at Central Park. She ended up next to Tara in the car. Stacy and Jake with his lucky penny were together in the back. She tried to give Tara a five-second driver’s need-to-knows, but her friend waved away the instructions. "I took driving lessons on the elfin world," she said.

Five minutes later, Lily regretted choosing Tara as the driver. Behind the wheel, she was a maniac. Sharp turns didn't bother her. Neither did traffic stops (STOP THE CAR!), squirrels on the road (hey, what's that furry thing over there?), or pigeons (aw, so cute - WATCH OUT!). People jumped to one side as the car swerved wildly on the road. But to be optimistic, they arrived at the park in one piece.

Stacy peeled herself off the back seat. "Can't we travel anywhere *safely*?" she groaned. Jake opened the door and staggered into the sunlight, holding his stomach. From the way he looked, Lily could tell he didn't approve of Tara's driving skills. "See? I did it," Tara said triumphantly.

Stacy gagged. "Tara, you *failed* your driving test." "Guys, calm down." Lily exited the car. Where was Sophie? The day was clear and bright, and yet there was no sorceress in sight. But suddenly the park turned eerily quiet, and Lily knew they weren't alone.

She turned to find Sophie charging at her, snarling. "GET THE COIN!" Lily shrieked. Jake fumbled the coin out of his pocket and threw it at her. As it hit the ground it turned into the cannon. Lily realized that there was nothing to light the long fuse. But then she got a closer look at the weapon. The long brown rope was coiled in a little circle, almost as though it were ... a button.

Lily slammed her fist down on the fuse and the cannon fired with a BAM. A silver blob of liquid metal fell on the grass and did nothing. *Great*, Lily thought. They had an AI blob on the grass that might possibly, just *possibly*, come to life. Two seconds later, the liquid puddle squirmed on the ground and came to life.

The blob flattened out on the ground and a figure rose out of it. Even Sophie stopped in her confusion, hesitating. A panther clawed its way out of the silver puddle and growled at Sophie. Jake whistled. "That's not a human." "That's a panther!" Tara yelled.

Sophie wrapped the panther in magic and it disappeared in a flash of gray light with a howl of surprise. For her next trick, she pulverized the cannon with a flick of her hand. The sorceress laughed. "I hold more power than all of you combined," she said, "and you would risk your lives to fight me?" She stomped her foot and gray mist collected in front of them, forming a giant ... pigeon.

The squawking bird solidified. It glared down at Lily with hate. "Pigeon!" Stacy shouted - which, by the way, doesn't get the same reaction as screaming "Shark!" The pigeon ruffled its gray plumage and screeched, a high and scratchy sound that set Lily's teeth chattering. "That is *not* good," Jake decided.

"Run!" Tara screamed. The bird squawked and moved at a surprisingly fast speed. Lily and her friends left the smiling Sophie behind and fled, climbing in the car with Tara at the wheel. As they barreled down the road with tires screeching, Jake said, "Well, I'm not going to visit that park ever again." "We're being chased by a giant member of the dove family, and you're thinking about a park?" Lily shouted.

SQUAWK! The pigeon chomped on the back of the car. Lily just hoped that she could find a decent excuse for her mother about the car. *Why is there a huge dent on my trunk? Oh, well ... we were being chased by a giant pigeon with a bad temper.* How truthful.

"Hold on!" Tara yelled. She swerved off the road, shot up a hill, and launched off it, sailing over a canal without bothering to find a bridge. Below them, a fishing boat sailed calmly in the water, as if the passengers onboard saw cars being chased by giant pigeons every day.

BANG! The car slammed into the curb on the other side. Unfortunately, the pigeon just flew over back to them. Lily hoped the vehicle wouldn't get any major injuries - a broken axle, perhaps, or a flat tire. Tara returned to the road. "We'll have to get to the highway!" she said. *Oh, no,* Lily thought. Stacy tapped her on the shoulder. "Um, the pigeon's gaining on us."

Lily looked into the mirror. The giant bird was very close to them now. Fortunately, car mirrors always said: OBJECTS APPEAR TO BE CLOSER THAN THEY SEEM.

Tara turned the car sharply into the highway and sped up. Other vehicles honked their horns and swerved as the pigeon wreaked chaos and destruction. Lily realized that they were rapidly speeding towards the New York border. She wanted to stay in the city.

"Brake!" Lily yelled. Tara stomped on the brake as Lily grabbed the wheel and turned it. The car screeched a full 180 degrees until it faced the huge bird. "Gas!" she shouted. The car zoomed forward, right under the pigeon, which promptly sat down on them.

That was unexpected. Lily had meant to speed back to the local area, but the pigeon snapped at the air and droppings sloshed over the windshield. Tara activated the wipers. In the back, Stacy and Jake gagged in disgust. "That's a bunch of crap!" Jake yelled.

The pigeon continued to use the car as a toilet. Stuck under its rear, Lily could only hope that the roof didn't cave in under the weight of dung. Tara pressed her hand to the horn hard and the bird momentarily flew up in surprise and confusion.

In that moment, Tara floored the gas and the car zoomed forward, dodging cars like crazy. "Left! Watch out for that car!" Lily screamed. "Pigeon's coming!" Jake said.

Soon they were back on the streets, the car covered in white crap. Tara steered the vehicle to Lily's apartment and they left it in the parking lot, leaving it for Lily's mother.

Lily called Theresa on her phone: "Theresa, just so you know, there's a giant pigeon on the loose that gave my mom's car a new paint job. Also, we could use some help with finding Sophie. Bye!"

Two minutes later, Lily and her friends found army-issued missile launchers appearing in their hands with a flash of gray light.

"Now that I think of it," Stacy said, "I feel sorry for the pigeon." They clambered back into their poop-covered car and sped off in pursuit of the pigeon.

Chapter 54

A certain giant pigeon gets attacked by army-issued missile launchers

The pigeon apparently lost interest in chasing their car. For the next ten minutes, it was nowhere to be seen (actually, everyone could only look through the front window because the other windows were covered in ... never mind). Eventually, they found the oversized bird ransacking the nearest Stop and Shop cereal aisle. Cheerio dust (Cheerios were all the rage with New Yorkers in 2037) covered its plumage as it munched happily. Again, there was no one in sight, no onlookers. Lily wondered if Sophie radiated a wave of fear - so strong, it left the citizens of New York City cowering in their homes.

Pushing that thought aside, she climbed out of the car with some difficulty, as the door was quite stuck with pigeon poop. Grabbing her trusty missile launcher, she ran to the nearest lamppost and hid, motioning for her friends to follow.

And there they were, a squad of armed teenagers (or so it looked) crouching behind a lamppost, rebellious against giant pigeons. Why not?

Lily hefted her launcher up and aimed it at the bird, and it fired with a BANG.

Chapter 54: A certain giant pigeon gets attacked by army-issued missile launchers

SQUAWK!!!!? The pigeon looked up and staggered (or should I say, *waddled*) backward, and the attack began. The missile sailed into the air and exploded next to the bird, causing it to fall on its side. It didn't seem particularly hurt, though, just very surprised and annoyed.

The giant pigeon got back on its feet, only to be assaulted by multiple airborne exploding projectiles as Lily and her friends fired their missiles with incredible accuracy. Unfortunately, Sophie must've used good magic to create the bird, because it never got many injuries - a few bruises, perhaps. The pigeon did send a few attacks to their side, though. Five minutes in, Jake got kicked into the lamppost.

The fight ended when Stacy sent a whole line of missiles at the poor bird's gray side. The pigeon squawked in disappointment and burst into a pile of large gray feathers.

Lily set down her missile launcher. She felt bruised and battered. That stupid pigeon had picked her up with its beak and thrown her into the wall, sending her sprawling. Ouch.

"We should find Sophie," Tara said, "before it's too late."

"Yeah." Lily picked up a feather and kicked the pile at her feet. "Let's go tell her we don't like her work."

They didn't get to Sophie.

They ended up absolutely nowhere driving around randomly, searching for the sorceress. Eventually, Lily told the others that it was getting late, and she called off the search and they headed for home.

That night Tara brought the car back to Lily's apartment. When she returned, Lily asked, "Did you tell my mother?" "No." "Thanks." Tara went off to her room.

Lily opened her giant fridge and got out some pizza. She stuck it into the microwave and sat on her bed. She was so tired, she just wanted to fall over, but she was also hungry for dinner. Also, she had learned a lesson all firefighters repeatedly told the kids at school: never *ever* leave a microwave or oven on and fall asleep.

So that's why ten minutes later, Lily was tiredly munching on a slice of pizza with the microwave safely on the counter. When dinner was finished, she collapsed on her soft, comfortable bed and fell asleep almost instantly.

A loud BANGBANGBANG jolted Lily from her sleep. She rolled out of bed and smashed into the floor. "Ow!" She dragged herself to the bed and managed to get to her feet. She sleepily wandered to the door and opened it.

"Lily?" Theresa stood in front of her, and she looked as if though she had gone through a big fight with her sister. Given the situation, Lily supposed that could've happened. "What could you possibly want at 3:00 AM?" "I wanted to talk, actually." Theresa pushed past Lily and sat down in the living room.

"So, what do you want to say?" Lily rubbed the sleep out of her eyes as she talked. Theresa leaned forward, her elbows on the table between them. "I snuck into Sophie's headquarters."

Lily tried not to look surprised. Sneaking into Sophie's lair was dangerous and daring - a bold move that only someone like Theresa could have done." "Did you get caught?" she said warily. "No. Yes. I mean-" Theresa sighed in exasperation. "Sophie *found* me and *attacked* me, but she didn't *catch* me." "And *what*, exactly, did you break into your evil sister's lair for?" Lily still thought what Theresa did was crazy, and she hoped the reason wasn't an attempt of a family reunion.

Theresa's eyes glittered. "I stole something." She reached into the pocket of her shirt (she had changed clothes) and slid a computer disk across the coffee table. "A recording. Of everything that Sophie's done that was evil, and why. I believe it would make for a decent super weapon."

Lily stared at it. "Why would you risk your life to get this?" "Because you are my friend." Theresa wrung her hands. "I *hate* Sophie," she said in a hoarse whisper. "When the war first began, I put you as my top priority, my worst enemy. But I had forgotten about my sister. When she came ... I realized that you had nothing to hold against me, that you were never my enemy until I attacked your friends."

Lily picked up the computer disk and held it in her fist. "If I see this, could I find Sophie?" Theresa nodded. "After all these years I've done in evil, I realized that I just couldn't watch another life-filled planet be destroyed."

"*Thank* you, Theresa," Lily said. "This means the whole world to me." Fatigue took over her body. "I should sleep. Can I get you something to drink?" The sorceress nodded. Lily made some coffee and gave it to Theresa before heading off to bed, setting Sophie's disk on the bedside table.

"Wait," Theresa called. Lily froze. "Yes?" "Sophie showed me something. Right before I escaped."

Lily turned around. "Show me," she said.

Theresa smiled. "I'll show it in your sleep." Lily instantly knew she was going to have some strange dreams.

Right before she fell asleep, she saw Theresa through the open doorway, staring blankly out the panoramic window as she sipped her coffee. Could she really be letting go of her wrongdoings? Before Lily fell asleep, she decided not to just list Theresa as an ally, but as a friend.

Chapter 55

Lily's dream

Five seconds after Lily closed her eyes, she started dreaming. Two figures appeared, attacking each other with blasts of gray light. Mist swirled around them in a wispy miniature tornado. In the back of her mind, Lily recognized them as the two sisters - Theresa and Sophie. The grappled over a slightly familiar grassy field pitted with craters. In the chaos and dark - they were fighting during the night - Lily couldn't tell who had the upper hand.

In the back, four people stood watching. They were Lily and her friends. As the battle intensified, Sophie sent a bolt of gray light coursing through Theresa. The sorceress fell, trailing gray mist. As Sophie stood triumphant over her hopefully only unconscious sister, Lily ran to Theresa's side.

Lily sat straight up in bed, frozen with terror and confusion. Daylight streamed through the windows. Theresa was nowhere to be seen. She checked her alarm clock: 7:00AM.

Lily fixed herself some breakfast. As she ate, she couldn't take her mind off the dream. She hoped it was just something Sophie sent to scare Theresa off (*not* likely, but still) but somehow it held the ring of truth. And Lily didn't think it was just an effective threat. She speculated that Sophie had shown her sister a glimpse of the future. If so, then Lily was sure the defeat of Theresa would lead to Doomsday.

She put her plate in the sink and snatched the computer disk off the bedside table.

Afterward, she paid a visit to Tara, who was eating her breakfast. She told her friend about Theresa in her room, and about the strange dream she'd had during the night.

Tara stared at the table. "So we're doomed, then?" "Not quite," Lily replied. She held up the computer disk and explained just how valuable it was.

"So all we need is a computer," Tara said. "Yes." Lily got up. "I want to read this as soon as possible. Because it'll take too much time to wake the others, I'll take you to my house. I have a computer in my room." "Why me?" Tara called after Lily as she left the room.

"Your room is closest to mine."

Chapter 56

The computer disk

Ten minutes later, Lily and Tara had caught up with a hoverbus and were waiting to get to Lily's apartment. Fortunately, the trip was quick, as the bus was efficient and, well ... hovering. When they arrived, Lily went up to her room and was almost knocked over by her brother. "Lily!" The 8-year old was giddy with excitement. "Hey, Peter." "Daddy at work," Peter said matter-of-factly. Lily picked up her little brother and swung him around. "Tara, this is Peter, my little brother," she said. Tara patted him on the head. "Can we go to your room now, Lily?" she asked. "Yeah," she replied. She turned in the direction of the kitchen and yelled, "Mom, I'll be in my room!"

When the two got to her bedroom Lily went to her desk, where her Apple computer sat. She turned it on and plugged the computer disk in. Tara closed the door. Lily got into her reader app and started to read the long account of Sophie. When she and Tara were done, she began to form a summary: Sophie Foveae was a woman set on a single goal: to be stronger and more powerful than her younger sister, Theresa. Her strength: almost unlimited power at her fingertips. Her weakness: that her magic would be stolen and Theresa would rise to a higher rank than her. Sophie had a headquarters located in Los Angeles, called The Misty Mansion. What a coincidence!

Lily took the computer disk out of her computer. "How long do you think it will take for us to get to LA?" she asked Tara. Her friend smiled. "Let's find out."

While Tara went back to get Jake and Stacy, Lily went back home, where her mom and Peter (her younger brother) greeted her. "I called your dad," her mom said. "How do you feel about visiting your uncle in Los Angles? Your brother will wait for your dad with a babysitter here." Lily said, "Awesome!" and headed to her room to pack. A week later, they set off for the airport. During the flight, Lily sent Theresa a quick text: *Uh, sorry to bother you, but we're heading to LA. If we need anything, send it to our pockets. Bye!*

The plane soared into the air. The plane heaved with turbulence, and Lily could hear poor Stacy in the seat behind her - getting ready to heave. Five minutes later, Stacy stood up. "I'll just be-" she pointed at the bathroom. "Yeah, sure." Lily reclined in her chair. Meanwhile, Jake was happily playing the latest version of Call of Duty on the small backseat TV. Lily set off on conquering Bejeweled 3 while Tara watched over her shoulder, giving advice.

A few hours later, the plane touched down at the LA airport. Everyone grabbed their luggage and walked off the aircraft. Lily's mom took them all to a hotel. "Ok, now all we have to do is find The Misty Mansion ... wherever that is," Lily muttered. "We need a ride," Stacy added. "Nah, we can walk," Jake countered. "No!" complained Stacy.

"Shut up," Tara snapped. Stacy and Jake stopped bickering immediately and looked at her. "Watch the expert do this." Tara calmly walked to the house nearest to the hotel and knocked lightly on the door. A kindly old woman opened the door. "What can I do for you, sweetheart?" she said.

Tara put on a warming smile. "Hello. We need a ride to The Misty Mansion." The old lady smiled right back. "Of course. Just one second!"

Soon Lily and her friends were cramped together in the back of a black Chevrolet with the old lady (her name turned out to be Emily) at the wheel, driving down a road clogged with traffic. Nevertheless, Emily made her way through while giving a running commentary about Los Angeles. "Over there is the LAPD department," Emily pointed.

Jake cleared his throat and looked out the window. It looked like he was attempting to keep a straight face. "That place looks interesting," he said. He pointed to a beautiful fountain in the middle of a spotlessly clean park. At the top, a tall and pretty stone woman knelt with a dazzling smile. Her arms were outstretched towards Lily. She was dressed in a flowing gown - and for some reason, she seemed vaguely familiar. With her hair tumbling down her shoulders, her smile seemed slightly cold and perhaps cruel, a smile that made Lily shudder.

Emily peered out the window. "That's a park, of course. The fountain is called the Fountain of Magic."

Lily looked back at her. She had recognized the statue. "Is that a statue of Sophie Foveae?" "Why, yes! Have you been to Los Angeles before?" "No," Lily said flatly. Emily returned the conversation to the Fountain of Magic. "There used to be this legend of a woman named Sophie Foveae. Rumors claimed she had magic, in the form of gray mist. She was considered a hero back in ancient times. But the stories also said that she went into hiding - after the first war." Tara leaned forward in her seat. "The first war?" she asked. "You mean ..." "You see, Sophie was not a human. A really long time ago, she and her kind went to war with another humanlike species. Sophie was the leader of her army. As the legends say, she had a general at her side as she fought - her younger sister, Theresa. With her sister watching her back, Sophie won the war ... but she did it for a price. Sophie was driven back from the front lines in the last few minutes. In the end, it was Theresa who led her army to victory. Of course, she had gray mist as her magic. Sophie got furious. She had a fear that Theresa would one day be more powerful than her. She banished her sister ... and then she disappeared."

Awkward silence rang in the air. Lily got an uncomfortable feeling in her stomach. "Emily," she said. "How do you know all this?" Emily looked in the rearview mirror and chuckled. "Sweetheart, I'm not human. I fought in the first war."

Chapter 57

Sophie's headquarters

Stacy, who had been looking at the floor, stared at her in shock. Lily did the same, looking up so fast she almost got whiplash. "Who are you and where did you come from?" she demanded. Emily smiled. "I used to be a human back then. I knew Sophie. We were best friends when we were young. Days before the war started, Sophie asked me for help, and I accepted. I fought well. It was me who alerted Sophie that Theresa was taking over. When the war ended, Sophie left almost immediately. But at the last minute, she pulled me aside. She thanked me for keeping my loyalty. She passed on some magic to me, just enough to stay young for a much, much longer time. But now the power has worn off, as you can see." Emily stared sadly at her aged hands. "We're here."

The car pulled up to the curb. A walkway led up to a mansion. Mist curled around its walls. "You must go," the old woman said. "Thank you," Lily replied. She and her friends exited the car. As Lily walked away, she heard the driver's door open and Emily's hand grabbed her wrist hard.

Lily whipped around. "Please," Emily said. "I can't let you go there. It's too dangerous." She sounded like Theresa. "I have to," Lily answered. "Then let me give you a few pieces of advice. Don't challenge Sophie to a duel. Don't speak her name, as it would alert her to your presence. And don't ever, *ever* get captured," the old woman said in a hoarse whisper. Lily watched as Emily closed the door and revved the car engine. She rolled down the window. "Good luck, sugar." She smiled and drove away, leaving Lily and her friends to walk away to their fate.

Lily took a deep breath. "Everyone ready?" she asked. Her friends gripped their luggage and nodded. "Then let's do this." They went down the walkway.

The first casualty: the door was locked. Fortunately, Theresa had sent tiny bags in their pockets that grew to full size as they took them out. Lily pulled an extra-strong laser cutter out of her bag and busted the lock. After that, she and the others took the stuff they needed, stashed their bags behind a shrub and entered Sophie's headquarters.

After walking around for thirty seconds, Lily decided that either Sophie was really rich, or she had good magic. Huge glass and diamond chandeliers hung from the ceiling, reflecting soft light off the gold walls. The floor was polished to the point of perfection. Giant red curtains were draped over the large windows. In other words, Lily considered the place *extremely* dangerous. But first things first, cut the lights.

Lily whispered, "Stick the dimmers on the walls." She had learned from Stacy that dimmers sent an electrical charge throughout the building - harmless to human beings, but the lights would fizz out like a bug zapper. They brandished their dimmer grenades and set to work as silently as possible, attaching them to every wall they could find in the room, activating the five-minute timer on every single one of them. When they were done, they crouched behind a velvet couch and waited.

Chapter 57: Sophie's headquarters

BZZZZZT! Lily winced as the electrical charge raced through the mansion and cut the lights. After a few moments in darkness, Stacy whispered, "Let's go." Luckily, Lily had explained their plan to the elves before they packed. She and the others got out their flashlights and got out from behind the couch.

The search dragged on. Occasionally Lily would hear a noise like someone was slipping between the marble columns that lined the walls. But when she shined her flashlight at the spot, there was nothing in sight, which just added to her growing fears. Soon the noises started happening more frequently. Lily realized that the sounds were heading towards the far wall, as though there was something important. Suddenly she knew that whoever was hiding in the dark couldn't reach that wall.

As fast as she could, Lily whipped out a net bomb, switched the net size to maximum, and chucked it at the wall. BOOM! She could hear the net lashing itself to the far wall and the sounds of the footsteps retreating. Next to her, Stacy whispered, "Where's Sophie?"

Big mistake. Instantly, the footsteps came in their direction. Stacy yelped and vanished, her flashlight falling to the ground. Lily heard Tara's and Jake's lights also hitting the floor. She was alone.

Lily backed up into the nearest wall, taking deep breaths so she wouldn't panic. She realized just how much she hated being in the dark. As she calmed down, a voice said, "Hello, Lily."

Lily was instantly alert. The lights flickered on, and the soft light seemed almost blinding. Sophie stood in front of her, and she couldn't help noticing how much the sorceress looked like the stone statue in the fountain. Behind her sat three screens. The leftmost one showed Tara, her back against the wall, a look of pure terror on her face as a dark shadow loomed over her. The middle screen revealed Jake dangling from the ceiling over a pit of black scorpions. The screen didn't have audio, but Lily could tell he was screaming. The last screen had Stacy on the floor, staring at the mechanical monsters slowly approaching her.

Sophie smiled. "Decide which two of your friends will be saved." Lily swallowed. Sophie was asking her a trick question. Her best friends, who had helped her through their numerous adventures ... and yet only two Sophie would let go. She recalled what Emily had said: *And don't ever,* ever, *let Sophie capture you.* Is this what she meant? The things that would happen to the one person that she didn't choose ...

Lily's mind came up blank as she tried to think of a plan. "I-I can't," she murmured. The sorceress shrugged. "Choose the two that I will let escape." Suddenly Lily had a crazy idea ... but only if the person in mind was listening. "Release Tara and Stacy," she whispered. "Hmm?" "Release Tara and Stacy!" Lily yelled. "Very well," Sophie said. Tara and Stacy disappeared from their screens.

Lily desperately thought, *Theresa, please, help.* She stared at Jake's screen. If her plan didn't work, he would be abandoned to Sophie with no chance of mercy. Sophie smiled and Jake started to fall.

It wasn't until Jake was halfway down to the scorpions that he realized what was going on. As he tried to stop his fall a jet of gray mist smashed into him, and he vanished. Sophie, whose back was to the screen, grinned triumphantly. Lily had to play up the act, or she would get suspicious.

"No!" Lily lunged at Sophie, but the sorceress blocked her attack easily. "How can you be so *cruel*?" she shouted. Since she was already terrified, it didn't take much to look horrified. Sophie smiled smugly ... and then a look of surprise, then horror, came across her face. "Dang it!" she whirled around as a torrent of gray mist slammed into her, and she disappeared. Theresa appeared in front of her. "Hold on!" she yelled, and Lily's vision turned dark.

Chapter 58

Theresa ruins a park

When Lily's vision cleared, she was standing in - you guessed it - the Very Annoying Park of Sophie's Magic Fountain. As usual, the park itself was in good condition as ever, but it was nighttime. The statue of Sophie in the fountain seemed to be glowing in the dark, illuminating her regal stone face. Lily hated it more every second.

BAM! Sophie materialized ten feet away from the statue. She was on the other side, so she couldn't see Lily. Lily inhaled sharply and searched the park for Theresa. She wasn't in sight. Lily climbed into the fountain with as little noise as possible and crouched behind the statue. She waited, though she wasn't sure what for. Was she waiting to be captured? Was she waiting for Theresa to save the day? Lily hoped it was the second option.

Lily peered over the hem of the statue's dress. "What-?" Sophie looked around her. Her eyes locked on the fountain, and Lily held her breath, trying to make herself as small as possible.

Sophie stepped toward the statue.

"Interesting," she muttered. Sophie studied the stone statue with interest, but she seemed slightly distracted. Lily heard the tiniest of splashes next to her. Theresa appeared. She held a finger to her lips and mouthed, *don't move, you idiot.* As Theresa glanced at her sister, her foot slipped.

Chapter 58: Theresa ruins a park

The resulting splash was faint, but Sophie heard. She began to walk toward the statue. Theresa's eyes flickered uncertainly. Lily knew that they needed a distraction, but it had to be good enough to actually outsmart Sophie.

Theresa solved the problem. She pressed both of her hands to the base of the statue and frost spread over it, covering it with a thin layer of ice. Sophie snarled. As Theresa covered the statue with more frost, Sophie began to shiver, hugging her arms close to her body as she backed away. Lily realized Theresa was using the statue to her advantage. Amazingly, the stone carving looked so much like Sophie herself that she was able to transfer energy from the stone to Sophie - which meant anything that Theresa did to the statue happened to Sophie.

"Gah!" Sophie vaporized the statue with her own comeback - a wave of heat so intense, the rock steamed and smoked. Luckily, the statue imploded along with the water in the fountain, so both Theresa and Lily were drenched before the heat could reach them. They tumbled out of the fountain. The pieces of the statue lay scattered around them, bubbling and setting the grass on fire in various places. Theresa dropped a few gallons of water over the smoking gray park.

Sophie growled. "Theresa," she said. "I am going to pick you up and toss you into my dungeon." Theresa sighed. "Sophie, you are such a bore. At least Lily and I have better ways of communication." Lily nodded enthusiastically. "Oh, yes. She texts me on my phone." Even then, it was hard to keep a cheerful face without lunging forward and punching Sophie.

Sophie laughed and waved her hand. Lily's friends appeared on the grass next to Lily. Stacy groaned. "Oh, not her again." In that moment, Sophie attacked, sending a crackling bolt of gray light flying at Theresa. Theresa just managed to block it with her magic. The two sisters exchanged deadly attacks of magic that lit up the whole park. Lily herded her friends away from the scene, being careful not to step on the melted bits of Sophie's statue. They watched from a distance. Lily knew she should help, but they didn't have any weapons.

As the light show (there were no other terms to call the intense battle) progressed, so did Sophie's powers. Blasts of gray light came more frequently, and Lily could tell it was all Theresa could do to keep her sister at bay.

"This isn't going well," Jake said. "I can tell," Lily grumbled. Theresa glanced over her shoulder. "Lily, go!" she yelled. "I can take care of ..."

In that moment, Sophie struck. Gray light streaked towards her sister. By the time Theresa turned around, the magic had slammed into her and she fell to the ground.

Lily had envisioned this happening from her dreams and worries. But seeing it happening was different. Barely pausing to think, she ran towards Theresa and knelt at her side. To her relief, Theresa was still breathing, her eyes were open, and she looked very annoyed. Sophie stood over them, glowering. "I have always been the powerful one, sister," she said. Lily tried to kick her, but the sorceress dodged with a light laugh. A small distance away, Lily saw Tara sneaking behind Sophie.

Chapter 58: Theresa ruins a park

Tara pounced, shoving Sophie to the ground. Sophie's laugh turned into a shriek, then a snarl. She morphed into a cloud of mist that seeped into the ground. Tara's expression was grim and unsatisfied. "She just left like that?" she asked. "Yes," Jake replied. "Ugh. Sophie is *so* annoying," Stacy muttered. Theresa struggled to her feet.

"Thank you," she said. "She would have overwhelmed me. But I cannot further assist you in fighting Sophie." "Why?" Lily demanded. The sorceress held her gaze. "Because this is your fight to complete, Lily, not mine. You should know that by now. But remember: control your weakness and do not let it control you. With that, Theresa jumped into the air, and suddenly she was a glowing gray falcon that squawked and flew into the night. "Well, so much for bravery," Lily grumbled. But then she heard a voice - Theresa's - inside her head that filled her with the fear of something bad to come. *Lily, beware. Sophie's worst attacks come in phases.* All around them, gray light erupted towards the sky, forming a cage that rapidly began to solidify. "Run!" Stacy shouted. Lily and her friends bolted for the street.

Chapter 59

Sophie's worst attack

They barely made it out of the cage.

The gray light flickered and shifted as it hardened. Lily and her friends raced towards the wall as it began to block all vision of the outside world. She was worried that they would slam into the wall and bounce off, but her fear and anger kept her running.

They hit the cage at full speed, passing through the solidifying material. Lily felt like she was running through a wall of glue. *Ugh*, she thought with a shudder of revulsion. She sprinted to the other side as the gray cage gave a loud CRACK and turned into white marble, cold and unforgiving.

Lily's friends grumbled in complaint and relief. "Well, *that's* over," Jake said. "Relatively easy-to-escape trap, but it's over." Lily looked around uncertainly, recalling Theresa's words of warning. "Sophie's worst attacks come in phases," she said aloud. Stacy peered into the darkness. "That might not have been Sophie's worst attack," she said.

Five seconds later, a cold laugh echoed around them, and suddenly Lily felt terribly dizzy and nauseous. Her vision blurred. In an instant, she and her friends were inside the marble prison, and the taunting laugh was echoing off the walls, loud and clear. *DID YOU REALLY THINK THAT I WOULD LET YOU GO THAT EASILY?* Sophie's voice rang in the air.

Chapter 59: Sophie's worst attack

Lily turned around, trying to get her bearings. The sorceress's voice seemed to come from every direction. "Lily, what can we do?" Tara looked at her as the ground shook with Sophie's laughter. And suddenly, looking at her friend, Lily realized her fear: that at the time she needed help most, her friends would turn away. Now, with Tara in front of her, asking to help, she felt a little better. She wasn't alone. She would *not* let her fear take over.

"Face the cardinal directions! The road should be north," she yelled to the others. She pointed in the direction in which she hoped the road was.

Jake and the others stepped into their assigned positions. Hopefully, when Sophie appeared, they would be ready ... unless she dropped on them from above - frightening, and highly unlikely. The sorceress ceased her laughing. Lily knew she was watching them and seeing what they would do next. But before they could actually do anything, the air in front of them shimmered, and four smoky, wispy gray images of Sophie appeared in front of each one of them.

Lily, who was at the west point (at least, that was what she thought) stared into the stone cold eyes of Sophie. She clenched her fists and silently told herself to stay calm. If they attacked now, with no weapons, it would be the wrong time. *Lily Claire, you should know by now that I do not give up easily*. The fuzzy images of the sorceress regarded her, their eyes glittering with malice. *I only seek after you because Theresa has grown fond of you and your friends. When she broke out of the palace, well ... that got my attention.* "Sophie," Lily said, trying to keep the quaver out of her voice, "by coming after me, you are endangering my home. Leave."

The misty figures spread their hands, and glowing balls of gray fire appeared in each palm. *As soon as I find Theresa, I will leave this planet if you wish. But you interest me, Lily. And so I will stay here until* you *leave.*

A thrill of horror shot through Lily as she realized Sophie's plan. The misty ladies raised their arms and began to throw fiery gray balls at them.

For one moment, Lily thought, *well, they're just mist ladies, so the gray stuff must be mist, too.* She imagined Theresa watching from far away with a smile on her face, saying: *sister, that's mist, you idiot!*

The gray fireball passed ten inches from Lily and slammed into the marble walls of the prison. When the smoke cleared, the stone was bubbling like it had reached boiling point. It was then that Lily realized that they were in trouble. "Scram!" she yelled. Fortunately, Sophie's worst attack was like a game of dodgeball, except extremely dangerous and with a bunch of smoke. Lily knew that she and her friends couldn't afford to take even one hit from those things. The smoke didn't bother her - it was actually just random gray mist - but the marble walls around them were becoming more and more heated, making a smaller space.

The misty Sophies moved around the prison, throwing their deadly weapons about every two seconds. Lily was tiring, and she could tell her friends were, too. *Maybe*, she thought, *the ladies would disappear when they were just at the point of collapse.* A moment after she had that thought, Stacy screamed, "Look out!"

Lily followed her instincts. She dove for cover - and just in time, too. A sizzling projectile flew over her and smashed into the wall. Tara screamed in rage and leaped at the nearest smoke lady, shoving her into the wall. The image dissolved with a soft hiss. Stacy slapped another into the wall and yelled, "The wall's our only chance of defeating these things!" It took a few more minutes for Jake and Lily to jump on the rest of the evil Sophies and destroy them. The marble walls disappeared with a *poof!*

Lily sat down on the grass. The others joined her. Lily thought for a while. "If I'm not underestimating how crazy Sophie is, she should be back by this morning." With the moon high in the sky, they caught a taxi and went home (or at least, the hotel). She marched to her room and shut the door, falling on the bed. Soon, sleep had taken over, and she fell into a chasm of dreams that made no sense.

First, she saw Tara sparring with Sophie in the middle of a deserted plain. Then her friend changed into Theresa, who screamed and shoved her sister to the ground. The scene changed to Jake looking at her grimly, who turned into Stacy, who said, "Beware, Lily. Sophie's worst attacks come in phases. Have you already forgotten Theresa's words?"

Lily's dreams shifted yet again to reveal an army of elves gathering at the summit of a high hill, their armor and weapons gleaming. Standing at the front was an unusually small elf, giving orders and shaking his fist. Lily willed her vision to zoom and she suddenly saw that the elf was not an elf after all, but a dwarf in disguise, no doubt one of Sophie's minions. Among the crowd stood Jake's older brother, Parker. Lily could see the coiled-up energy in his body, ready to pounce. From his strangely angered expression, Lily could tell he knew the short 'elf' was not on their side. His hand was tight on his sword hilt. His eyes flickered uncertainly around him and Lily realized what Parker was thinking: the damage was already done. If he attacked, his allies would try to stop him.

Lily watched as Parker unsheathed his sword, and the dream dissipated altogether.

Lily woke up with a start. Sunlight streamed through the open window. Jake Iander stood at the doorway, his face perplexed. "The elves have come. Hundreds of them," he said. "They've been tricked," Lily said. "Your brother is among them. But I think he's still on our side." "What do you mean?" Jake asked. "What about all the other elves?" Lily shook her head. "It's too late for them. A dwarf snuck into their ranks and pretended to be their leader. I had a dream about it."

"But what-?" Jake stumbled backward as the building shook. Lily could hear the clamoring and yelling of people outside the hotel - and it seemed like a lot of people.

Lily got out of bed and ran past her mother, who stood pale at the door. With her friends following, she sprinted down the hall and took the stairs to the door. Holding her breath, she unlocked the door and yanked it open.

She found herself looking into the eyes of more than two hundred elves. Confusion spread through their ranks as they stared at her. Lily tried to smile. "Hello." A young elf stepped forward. He held his sword tight in his hand. "We were told Sophie was in this city of Los Angeles," he said. "Well, she's not." Lily scanned the crowd. "I haven't seen her since last night."

But the elf shook his head. "It is too late. There are several hundred more elves in four other separate groups scouring the city in search of

Sophie." The gears in Lily's head began to turn. "She wants to separate you," she insisted. "We have to find the others." The confused army obligingly parted to let Lily through and she led them throughout the city with the help of a map from the leader of thc group. She managed to find all the other elfin groups in the park. Fifty yards away she heard a voice: *Lily, I come for you*. "Oh, that's not good," Stacy murmured.

"CLOSE RANKS!" Lily's voice carried over the elves easily and the group behind her marched across the road and stood shoulder to shoulder with the other army as the grass and trees in the park withered away to dust that scattered in the air. Tara snatched a sword from the nearest elf and brandished it. Lily did the same. Sophie appeared, holding a sword of her own, the blade honed to a deadly edge. She smiled. "Welcome, my dears. Would any of you care for a little combat?"

Chapter 60

A peculiar invasion

Sophie raised her sword, and armed dwarves appeared in a flash of blinding gray light, charging upon the surprised elves with cries of battle. In a few moments, the park was a maelstrom of fighting elves and dwarves. Tara leaped forward and began sparring with Sophie, their weapons moving so fast they were impossible to follow. The two dodged and parried with the battle raging around them. Lily noticed that the dwarves and elves alike kept a wide distance from the swinging blades.

Lily ran through her list of sword tricks and used them on her enemies, wading through the crowd and slowly making progress towards Sophie. Jake, who had gotten a dagger, crept up behind Sophie. But the sorceress was on high alert. Tripping Tara, she whipped around and knocked Jake's blade out of his hands, kicking him backward. Jake fell, and Sophie swung her weapon at him.

"No!" Parker appeared out of the crowd, knocking his brother aside as the sorceress's sword grazed Jake's arm. They tumbled into the raging battle and disappeared. Tara had gotten up and was busy whacking a group of heavily tattooed dwarves. Lily lunged at Sophie with her sword drawn.

It was a good thing Lily was fast. She barely managed to block Sophie's first attack and the fight began. They traded attacks back and forth, faster and faster. Lily ducked and Sophie tripped her. She landed hard on the ground. Sophie stomped on the dirt and a magical gray charge flowed through the crowd, surrounding every dwarf. Sophie's minions seemed to stand up straighter (but because they were, you know, *short*, they didn't get much height difference) and they started attacking with renewed energy. Lily got to her feet unsteadily.

From the moment she had fallen, the massive crowd had surrounded her in their fight, obscuring all vision and forming a wall from Sophie. Nearby, she saw a young girl dashing through the chaos, dodging weapons and carrying a first aid box - Oneida, doing her job as a nurse. Lily ran to meet her.

"Oneida! What are you *doing* here?" Lily followed Oneida to a place out of the battle. "There were no other nurses who would come," Oneida said. "But ..." Lily heard the unmistakable sound of several bowstrings being drawn taught. "Duck!" She tackled Oneida as a line of dwarves simultaneously fired a wave of arrows at them. Several pierced the ground inches from Lily. The rest sailed into the air harmlessly. As the dwarves reloaded several dozen elves fell upon them. Lily got to her feet, snatching up the first aid box from the ground and placing it in Oneida's arms. "Don't drop it," she said sternly. Oneida nodded and sprinted behind a tree, where elves immediately ran towards her carrying the wounded. Lily sidestepped them all and ran back into the battle.

And so it went. Lily fell into a sort of trance, striking with her sword and trying to make her way to Sophie, who stood in the middle of it all. She managed to get within five feet from the sorceress, but before she could strike, Sophie disappeared.

"What-?" Lily turned in a circle and saw Sophie close by, still fighting. She tried to approach the sorceress again, but Sophie vanished and appeared somewhere else. Lily realized that she was teleporting herself away from Lily every time she sensed her coming.

She decided to not attack.

Instead, Lily focused on the bigger and less dangerous targets - the dwarves. By now the afternoon sun was high in the sky, but Lily could tell Sophie sent out a danger vibe to keep people in their houses. Lily set to work, knocking the weapons out of the enemies and kicking them over. Just as she was about to sneak up on another dozen dwarves, she tripped over someone lying on the ground. She looked down. "Jake!"

Jake lay sprawled at the edge of the battle with a long cut on his arm from when Sophie hit him. Lily dragged him over to Oneida, trying her best to dodge flying weapons. Depositing him next to his sister, she turned and found herself face to face with Stacy. "What is it?" Lily said. "I found something." Stacy's eyes gleamed. "You better check it out."

Chapter 61

A cavern of dragons

Stacy led Lily to a cavern opening several yards away from the battle. It was lit with a soft orange light. Lily went in with her sword drawn. Stacy kept her hand rested on the hilt of her sheathed sword. As Lily cautiously walked down the tunnel, the air seemed to get warmer. Soon the heat was making the walls steam. Lily felt as though she and Stacy were walking towards the sun. The tunnel gave a sharp right and opened up into a cavern. Lily looked up and inhaled sharply.

Dragons. Hundreds of them, roaming around aimlessly and breathing fire.

"What *are* they?" Lily asked. "At first glance, I'd say they're dragons. But dragons don't live on this planet," said Stacy.

Lily wiped her sweaty hands off on her pants. The temperature seemed to boost up ten degrees every time a dragon breathed a flaming column of fire towards the cave ceiling.

She held her sword at arm's length and approached the nearest dragon, which was snoring loudly on the floor. It was a gray-yellow dragon, and like the rest of its brethren, it was wingless. Lily poked it hard with her sword and the dragon disappeared with a *poof*! Lily glanced down. Lying at her feet was a very cute stuffed dragon, barely bigger than her hand, with oversized eyes that stared scornfully at her.

She kicked the toy and it rolled over the stone floor. "This has to be the weirdest joke Sophie's ever played on us." "Agreed," Stacy replied. Lily prodded the stuffed animal with her sword in disbelief and a high-pitched scream emitted from its closed mouth. Lily glanced up. "Uh-oh." Apparently, she had caught the attention of every single dragon in the cavern. As the toy continued to scream, a dragon opened its mouth and incinerated the stuffed animal with a well-aimed jet of white-hot fire. Lily had a feeling her sword wouldn't make a dent in any of the dragons, much less turn them into an adorable stuffed animal.

The dragons roared and charged towards them. "RUN!" Lily yelled. She and her friend sprinted back down the corridor from which they came from. Lily hoped that the tunnel would be too narrow for the dragons. No such luck. She heard the rumbling and grinding of stone as the dragons busted their way through. A new sense of fear filled her and she grabbed Stacy's hand, pulling her out of the tunnel into fresh air.

"Go, go, go!" Lily herded Stacy back into the battle. Suddenly, there was a loud BOOM and the dragons charged out of the cavern opening. Both sides stumbled backward as the giant creatures shouldered their way through. Lily shoved elves and dwarves aside, catching Tara's arm on the way and dragging her along. She and her friends tumbled behind a tree next to the medical area just as the dragons charged past, roaring and kicking up a dust storm that made everyone cough.

Tara sneezed. "What *are* those?" Lily shrugged. "Don't know. Dragons?"

A stray dragon lumbered after its brethren and sprayed fire at them, causing Jake to scoot backward. "That's a dragon," he said. "Yes, yes, we all know, Jake. Don't worry, it'll be fine," Lily answered impatiently. Jake stared after the roaring beasts as they rampaged. "But they're *dragons*," he insisted. Oneida sighed, scooted over to Jake, and slapped him. "Ow!" he complained. "We *know* they're dragons, and we *can* take care of it," she said crossly. Jake pressed his back against the tree and said nothing. Oneida went away to care for the other patients as Lily surveyed the damage. Dozens of elves and dwarves lay on the dirt in the dragons' wake. About half of them were groaning, and most of the rest were whimpering and staring at the sky. Unfortunately, about a dozen looked very, very flat. Lily tried not to look at them and pulled her friends (except for Jake, of course; he was injured) away from the tree, where they made a mad dash for the dragons, clutching their weapons.

Tara and Stacy pounced on the first two dragons, but their blades slipped off the beast's scaly hide with no luck. "DON'T BE STUPID!" Lily yelled. "Find the chink in the armor!" *The chink in the armor.* Lily had no idea where the chink would be, but she approached a dragon anyway, the stray one that had blown fire at them. It growled and glared at her. As it shifted, she saw what she supposed was the chink - a tiny gap where one of the scales had come loose. She ran towards the dragon and plunged her blade into the chink.

The dragon shrieked with anger and pain, but it was losing strength. Clearly delirious with the pain, it stumbled backward, away from Lily's sword. She gripped it tighter. Lily wielded her sword and swung it at the dragon. *Thud.* The beast collapsed and fell against another dragon.

Lily took a deep breath and tried to focus. The chink, she realized as she fought, was not always in the same place. So she randomized her attacks, swinging at the holes in the scales, under the wings and at the tail. The other elves joined her, hundreds of them attacking the monsters. But she and her friends were tiring, and the dragons were multiplying. Every now and then Tara ran up to her to say important news: Jake was fighting again, Stacy had been knocked unconscious and was being treated, etc.

Lily stumbled and found herself face to face with a dragon. She took it down and whipped around. There was a sound that was so familiar ... but it shouldn't be occurring. Lily saw something near the road ... and muttered, "Crap."

Chapter 62

When things get worse

It was noon, and the city of Los Angeles had woken up.

Naturally, there was the confusion before the chaos. Undoubtedly, people had risen out of bed hearing screams, the clanging of metal, and the occasional roaring. What they thought was causing the commotion, Lily could never guess. A movie in the making?

Anyway, several hundred ordinary people had gone out for their morning walks and to get to work. Just so it happens, the park (which was the battlefield) was directly in the center of the metropolitan area, with the perfect amount of open space for the morning walk. In fact, everyone who took their walks went to the park. How convenient - and unfortunate. So the first two hundred or so people came out of their homes refreshed and ready for the day only to find out - ta da! - the park was filled with dragons and screaming armed people, half with pointy ears and half who looked very, very small. Not exactly your best wake-up call.

If Sophie had sent out a danger vibe, it hadn't worked long.

Lily had watched way too many action movies when she was a kid to imagine the chaos that was about to happen. And she was right. The people started to shriek and scream and call the police. And of course, they were all running away. To make things worse, the dragons, who preferred to be in open spaces so they could easily spot running targets, all charged after them. So now two hundred people were being chased by one thousand dragons who were being followed by a mix of two thousand dwarves and elves whacking each other with their favorite weapons. Lily sighed. Grabbing her friends (which included a very dazed Stacy), she dashed after the chaos.

The rampaging chaos had flowed onto the roads, causing a major traffic jam and of course, more screaming. The honking of horns collided with the rest of the racket to create an absolutely ear-splitting noise. The dragons roared and started to flip cars over. "Spread out," Lily told her friends. Since she and her friends were at the end of the crowd, she attacked as many dwarves as she could to make it easier to get to the dragons.

All around Lily, people were screaming, sirens were wailing, dragons were roaring - and annoyingly, Sophie was nowhere to be seen. Lily tried to assure herself that the sorceress had run away in fear and wasn't watching over them and adding new monsters to the battle. In fact, she tried not to think about Sophie at all. *Don't think about her*, she told herself. *She's not going to cause the apocalypse. Don't think about Sophie ... too late.*

Lily tried to shake all thoughts of the evil sorceress out of her mind and focused on the problem at hand. Her sword wasn't of much use on attacks up close, so the best she could do was defend herself. Her friends seemed to be having the same problem. The unusual roar of gunfire startled her.

The police had arrived. Hundreds of officers drove up in their shiny cruisers and filed out, screaming orders into walkie-talkies and fumbling to load their weapons and doing whatever else it is that frightened policemen do. Helicopters soared overhead, firing at the dragons, which was useless since the bullets bounced right off the dragons' hard scales. Lily hated the thought that the police were wasting good weaponry on the dragons. She sheathed her sword and ran towards the police officer that seemed to be screaming the most orders. "You need better weapons to defeat those creatures! Can you stop the helicopters?" she yelled.

The officer looked at her, a fifteen-year-old girl with her hair in her face and a sword at her side, giving him orders to stop an attack. "And why should I trust you, miss?" he said. That simple question utterly stumped Lily. He was right; why should *she* be trusted? "Um ... because you can?" The officer was outright stubborn. "Sorry, but I'm the one who's giving orders, not you," he said crossly. Just then, several dwarves charged towards them, hollering and swinging axes. Lily stepped forward, knocked the weapons out of their hands, swung her sword, and in several seconds, the dwarves were flat on the ground. As Lily turned back, a dragon swiped at her and barely missed, so she had no further time to chat. She looked over her shoulder and snarled, "Just do it!" at the officer. Lily dodged the dragon's razor sharp claws and disappeared into the crowd.

Chapter 63

How to ride a dragon (not for kids!)

Lily wasn't sure if her plan would work. She tried to be optimistic and hoped for the best.

Lily's goal was to get to somewhere more quiet and find some way to contact Theresa without getting seriously hurt or chomped by a dragon. She used her sword as a sort of shield/whacker to bat screaming dwarves out of her way. Unfortunately, pushing your way through this kind of chaos was like trying to run through water - it's tiring, and there's a lot of resistance from the water pushing you back. Soon Lily's legs were aching from kicking so many dwarves, and she was only about one-third through the crowd.

That's when things got a lot harder. Apparently, the dwarves had brought a few surprises with them. Those *surprises* meant two big fat grenades that simultaneously detonated five hundred feet away from Lily.

The shockwave from the blast threw Lily backward, and she landed hard on something hard, scratchy, and scalding hot. "Oof!" When Lily groggily regained her senses, she realized she was above the ground. To be precise, she was about thirty feet from the asphalt, having landed on the scaly sun-baked back of the very dragon who had swiped at her fifteen minutes ago. Luckily, there were no armed helicopters above her, or she'd be in big trouble. She stared at the raging battle below her ... and noticed something strange. Had the dwarves come into the battle with rainbow armor? She didn't think so. Then she saw Tara with a paintball gun, firing into the dwarves' offensive line ... which was basically every single little screaming person she encountered. All those poor people who had gone out for their morning walks had been gathered by the police into one shaking group, taking shelter in the nearest building.

Lily realized that it might be a good idea for Tara to be with her. But it isn't easy to climb up thirty feet of warm, moving dragon. Lily's case was exceptional, and she didn't want one of her friends to be going through *that* again. Unless there was a different way ...

Lily closed her eyes, feeling nauseous, and thought, *Theresa!* The reply came back almost immediately: *Lily, what do you need?*

I need Tara here, Lily answered. *Can I speak to her?* A flickering gray image of Tara appeared sitting on the dragon's back next to Lily. "Lily, what on earth are you doing up there?" she demanded. "Um, I kind of got ... blown here?" Lily replied. "Anyway, listen. Tara, I need you up here next to me." Lily told her friend the plan.

The hologram clutched her misty paintball gun uneasily. "I think I can follow your orders." "Don't say you *think* you can do it. Be more optimistic," Lily scolded. A faint smile came across Tara's shimmering face as she vanished.

Fortunately, Tara was close to Lily's location, so it didn't take her long to get dangerously close to the dragon. "Ready?" Lily shouted. Tara slid her paintball gun into her belt and nodded. Lily took a deep breath, crawled as fast as she could to the dragon's head, and swung her foot at the dragon's eye.

The effect was immediate. Humans do not like being poked in the eye. Turns out, neither do dragons. The beast roared in surprise and waved its tail wildly as Lily hung on for dear life. The tail swung straight towards Tara ... and she jumped.

Lily watched as Tara landed hard on the dragon's tail and held on, slowly inching her way up as she swung wildly. Eventually, she made it to the dragon's back and scrambled across to Lily. "What's the plan?" she asked breathlessly. Lily ignored the question. "Where'd you get the paintball shooter?" Tara grinned mischievously. "I kind of ... raided a toy shop. That dragon blew the shelves apart. Anyway, grab a paintball gun!"

Lily reached out and caught a paintball gun as it sailed towards her. She pointed it at the battle below and hesitated. "You know, this makes me feel a lot younger." Tara smiled.

Chapter 64

Paintballs!

Lily never thought fighting a battle could be fun. Paintballs changed the entire experience.

She and Tara sat at the base of the dragon's neck, shooting rainbow paintballs at dwarves. Occasionally they would hit an elf, but that was quickly taken care of. Lily did *accidentally* hit Jake with a paintball, though. That got a few laughs out from her, but she returned to being serious - at least, as serious as she could be while having a paintball fight. Turns out, paintballs were actually a good weapon choice. Soon, the dwarves had been reduced to mere hundreds.

It was around that time that Lily and Tara ran out of paintballs. Having fired their last rainbow projectiles into the dragons' eyes, they tossed their paintballs over their shoulders and drew their swords wearily. "Whoo!" Tara exhaled loudly and collapsed on the dragon's back. "That was extremely tiring. Can we please get off this ride?" Lily agreed, and so they slid down the dragon's tail and re-engaged with the battle. Stacy stumbled over. "Hey," she said breathlessly. Tara caught her as she keeled over. "Whoa, hold on, Stacy," she said. "I'm fine. I'm just a bit ... tired," Stacy mumbled.

Concerned, Lily felt Stacy's forehead. "I think she has heat stroke," she said to Tara. "Better get her somewhere shady and safe." Tara left, half carrying and half guiding Stacy away from the battle. Lily blamed the overwhelming heat on her exhaustion. But at least she could still fight. She didn't know how long she'd been in the battle until she began to get hungry. She ate a huge dinner last night, but it was probably around 2:00 PM. But it wasn't up to her to end the battle.

Five minutes later, Lily was battling yet another dragon when she heard a woman scream, loud and full of rage. She was vaguely aware of the dragon's shadow getting darker, and she dived out of the way, the dragon crashing dead on the asphalt seconds where she'd been before, a sword in its back. Lily rose unsteadily, only to be blasted off her feet by another grenade. Lily's ears rang as she crouched, dizzy and disoriented. Someone was yelling something in her ear, but Lily was too groggy to either hear or see the speaker. Struggling to remain conscious, she was yanked roughly to her feet. Lily cried out. She'd sprained her ankle as she fell. She gasped as her ankle twisted under her weight.

"Lily. Can you hear me?" Lily forced herself to look up and found herself staring into Theresa's eyes. The sorceress gripped her hand, and Lily felt the pain go out of her ankle. "You must flee," Theresa commanded. "I overheard Sophie talking to one of the dwarf generals. In about ten minutes, she'll cut the life sources on all the dragons and the dwarves will sink into the ground and disappear, transported to a prison under her home. Any other being in contact with a dwarf at that time will vanish with them." "So ... what do I do?" Theresa's eyes sparked with the old impatience she used to possess. "You should know. Run. Get out of the area and off the battlefield. Gather your friends and go." With that, she vanished.

Lily gulped. She was extremely keen not to get captured. She began to push warriors out of her way, gathering her friends as she sprinted past them.

Chapter 64: Paintballs!

With two minutes left on the clock, Lily grabbed Oneida's hand. She now had all her confused friends next her, but now what? They still had one-third of the crowded battlefield to cross. So she did the only option left. After telling her friends the plan, she jumped up and began to run over the dwarves' helmeted heads, careful to avoid the things that could trip her - which, in this case, were the elves' heads. They leaped off and ran away from the crowd just as the dwarves started to disappear, starting from the back.

As the shockwave quickly progressed, she saw someone else running over the dwarves' heads and heard Jake cry out in alarm. In all the confusion, she'd forgotten to grab Parker. And now he was racing in front of the shockwave, dwarves and elves vanishing inches behind him as he sprinted towards them. Jake stepped closer to the dwarves and stretched out his hand towards his brother. Parker grabbed it and they both tumbled to the ground as the last of the dwarves and elves disappeared with surprised screams, leaving no trace of the battle except for the dragon bodies lying limp on the road.

Parker doubled over, gasping for air as Oneida fussed over him. Lily blew the hair out of her face and saw that someone was running between the dead dragons, brushing her hand across their massive eyelids, white-blond hair flying out behind her. Lily knew who it was before she drew her sword. Her arm moved on its own, and the next thing she knew, the weapon was spinning towards Sophie like a boomerang.

When the blade was ten feet away, Sophie's eyes shot up for one second, but that was enough. She thrust out her hand and the sword rebounded off her glowing palm, spinning straight back at Lily, who yelped and ducked as the weapon embedded itself in a nearby tree.

Sophie brushed her fingers over the last dragon's eyelid and vanished into the air. The dragons groaned and stirred, wings sprouting from their backs, and soon they lifted off from the ground and disappeared into the clouds. "What are we going to do about *that*?" Stacy asked. "Um ..." Lily thought hard for a few seconds. "We watch the news and see what happens."

Chapter 65

The news

Lily didn't get to watch the news.

Turns out, her mother was very, *very* picky and sincerely concerned about the dangerous commotion going on. So while Lily was out on 'important business', her mom was packing up everyone's stuff. By the time Lily returned to the hotel, the plane was only an hour away from takeoff. After a ton of protests, Lily dismissed her friends to pack up and stomped off to her room, dozing off on the bed next to her suitcase.

A half hour later, her mom was telling her to wake up so they could catch the bus. Lily grabbed the most filling snack she could find in the fridge, scooped up her suitcase, and followed her mom out of the door. Her friends emerged from their rooms carrying their luggage. Oneida was rattling on to her two older brothers about how they had 'gone into battle with no armor and didn't watch out carefully enough' (actually, she was directing those words to Jake, while Parker smugly watched). The moment Oneida saw Lily's mother, though, she shut up. They left for the bus in silence, with Jake helping Parker lift up his heavy suitcase with armor inside.

Lily fell asleep on the plane. When she woke up, the plane was touching down in New York City. The instant Lily stepped inside her apartment room, she went straight into her bedroom, shut the door, and turned on the TV.

The news reporter was saying: “And now we turn to Melissa Gracie for more information.” “Thanks, Peter. Now, I’m standing in San Francisco, where people have repeatedly called the police, claiming they sighted a dragon causing destruction throughout the city. The same thing happened in the following areas: Los Angeles, Greece, Italy, Germany, Russia ...” Melissa rambled on from a long list in her hand. With each name, Lily’s dread grew. Someone behind her cleared his throat. Lily jumped and whipped around.

Lily’s friends had sneaked up on her. “Gah! You guys surprised me,” she exclaimed. Tara and Stacy both kicked Jake, who apparently was the one who had cleared his throat. “Ow!” he complained. Lily rolled her eyes. “Thank you, Jake, for ruining a perfectly terrifying moment.” “You’re very welcome,” Jake grumbled.

Dinner was silent. Lily’s mom tried her best to cheer things up, smiling at everyone and commenting on everything. Lily and her friends poked at their food with their forks and said nothing. When Lily’s mom had gone to sleep, Jake said, “Can Theresa send my siblings home?” Parker punched Jake in the arm. “Bro, seriously! What do you think the elves are going to say if I return with no one but my sister and say everyone else got imprisoned by Sophie?”

Oneida pushed back her empty plate. “Parker’s right. Jake, when we return, we might be shamed for leaving our allies undefended and open to Sophie’s attacks.” “Theresa can take care of it,” Lily said quietly. And even as she said those words, the sorceress appeared at her side. “I overheard your conversation,” she said. She looked at Jake’s siblings.

"Are you ready?" Parker and Oneida nodded reluctantly. "Okay, then. Let's go." Theresa took hold of their hands and they disappeared.

Stacy stood up and collected the plates, carefully setting them in the sink without a word. "Jake, if they do get shamed ..." "I am sure my brother and my sister will be able to work it out," Jake said tightly.

The awkward silence that followed was too much for Lily to bear. "Guys, that's not our main problem - Sophie is, remember?" Her friends nodded reluctantly. "And now that Jake's siblings are safe, we can all sleep a little easier. And-" Lily was about to say that they were probably doomed, but her voice caught in her throat. "And it's almost midnight," she managed. "So we should get some sleep." Stacy, Tara, and Jake said their goodbyes and left for the hotel, closing the door behind them. Lily sighed, turned off the kitchen light, and trudged down the hallway, where her bed awaited her. She knew *she* wasn't going to sleep any easier.

Chapter 66

There's a dragon outside the window!

Lily rose from a restless sleep highly alert, looking around her bedroom. As she'd woken up, she had sensed something close by, breathing loudly. Puzzled, Lily opened the window to welcome the sunny day and almost immediately closed it again.

There was a dragon outside her window. It was staring straight ahead with a bored look on its gray face. But it wasn't the sight that made Lily slam the window closed: it was the downright disgusting odor of sweaty dragon that choked her. How long had the dragon been sitting outside her apartment? Five minutes? Five *hours*?

Lily found herself calling Tara – apparently, she had stolen an iPhone along with the paintball gun during the battle. Tara answered the call immediately: "Lily, it's ten in the morning. Why are you calling me?"

Lily ignored the question. "What are you doing?" "Having breakfast with Stacy and Jake in my kitchen." "Great. Listen. I'm in big trouble."

"And how exactly are you in big trouble?" Tara asked impatiently. "There's a *dragon outside my window*, okay? Sophie must've tracked me down."

From what Lily knew about her friend's personality, Tara was either rolling her eyes or panicking. Probably the first option - no, *definitely* the first option. "And why should I be worrying about that?" Tara inquired calmly. "Because, um ..." Lily's voice petered out as she noticed some background noise: the sound of a window opening, and then Jake's voice screaming, "THERE'S A DRAGON OUTSIDE THE WINDOW!" Moments later, Stacy broke the awkward silence. "Shut up, Jake, and don't say things like that while I'm eating!"

Apparently, girls could handle pressure a *lot* better than boys (at least, compared to Stacy and Tara handling pressure next to Jake). Lily heard a long burst of static and realized that Tara was sighing. "If it's *that* bad, I suppose I should check it out. If you can't get out, try getting out through the fire escape. I'll see you at the library unless something really bad happens - like the dragon eating the toilet, for example." A loud CRUNCHsloshSPLASH noise erupted from the phone. Lily stepped back in surprise, pressing her ear to the phone just in time to hear Jake wailing, "THE DRAGON ATE THE TOILET!"

Tara was definitely sighing into the phone again. "Well, if I can still get out of the hotel without paying for the damage in my hotel room and Jake's very obnoxious screaming, I'll see you at the library." "Tara, who are you calling?" Stacy's voice emitted through the phone, followed by a loud thud - Tara must've dropped the phone. Seconds later, Lily could hear Tara's voice yelling, "Oh, *that* is *not* good. Get out! GET OUT!" Tara said into the phone, "Lily, if you haven't hung up yet, the dragon just ate the whole bathroom and flooded the kitchen with toilet water. Bye."

Lily hung up and peered out the window to find that the dragon was still there. She would have to risk the fire escape anyway; her bedroom window was several floors above the front door, which meant she would come out facing the dragon's ... butt. Lily shuddered, stuffing her phone in her pocket as she dashed out the door. Five seconds later, she rushed back in, snatched her suitcase of *special* equipment from the far corner of the room, and ran back out again. With her luck, when the dragon attacked, her mother would remember the evacuation protocol. Then a thought occurred to her: her mom was already at work.

Ten minutes later, Lily yanked open the fire escape door before remembering that this newly installed fire escape stairway was faulty and led right to a door five feet away from the main entrance. She abandoned the stairs and headed for the older fire escape - a rickety old series of metal platforms attached to the wall with rusty ladders that had to be pulled down. Unfortunately, the metal platforms were only about two feet in width and forty years of no use had left the ladders creaky and squeaky.

Lily stared down at the thirty-foot drop from her current location to the ground: head height for a sitting dragon. She took a deep breath and tossing her suitcase onto the platform below she began the long and dangerous task of climbing down the fire escape. She shinnied down the rusty ladder and almost tripped over her suitcase, barely managing to grab the ladder before she fell. Did I forget to mention there was no rail to hold on to? As it was, Lily handled the problem as carefully as she could by unsteadily regaining her balance.

She worked her way down the fire escape, trying not to look down. Two rusty platforms later, as Lily was about to drop her suitcase on the next platform a loud ROAR cut through the air, setting her teeth on edge. Seconds later, the building shook violently, sending plaster dust flying. Lily lost her grip on the ladder and fell. Her suitcase absorbed the worst of the impact as she crashed into the asphalt. Lily ran as her apartment creaked and groaned. People flooded out of the front doors as the highest levels of the apartment began to crack and break away.

The weight of Lily's suitcase was dragging her down, wasting her energy. But the contents were precious equipment: she couldn't let it fall into the wrong hands. Lily decided to keep the suitcase where it was, crammed under her arm. No, she wasn't going to abandon it. After what seemed like an eternity of running, Lily finally spotted the tall brick building that was the library. Stacy and Jake had apparently ducked into an alley and were now peeking out at her as she sprinted towards them. Tara stood directly in front of the library's front door, her hand outstretched. But there was something on her friend's face that confused Lily: the look of desperation and fear that made her run faster. Then she became aware of a rumbling sound, getting louder.

Lily lunged forward and grabbed Tara's hand. Tara pulled her roughly into the alley to dodge the dragons that plowed into the library. The old structure fell apart in a mess of bricks and books. Lily peered into the wreckage from the shadows of the alley before remembering that there was nobody inside - the library was closed on Sundays. The dragons plowed through the rubble and disappeared down the street as they took a sharp right.

Jake sniffed indignantly. "I've never liked books much, but ..." "If you want to read a book *now*, Jake, just do it, there're books everywhere," Lily said impatiently. Stacy kicked a squashed book out of the way. "We're not safe here," she said. "Let's move."

They made their way across the wreckage and walked away from the sirens and what was left of the library as Tara told Lily what happened before. "So, after the dragon ate the bathroom and flooded the kitchen, it started treating the entire hotel as ... as, well, a snack. Everyone got out safely. Jake was shaking like a leaf the whole time." "Hey!" Jake protested.

Stacy's eyes locked on her suitcase. "What's inside the suitcase?" Lily opened her bag, revealing the equipment inside: her sword, twelve shockwave grenades, one shrinkable shield, and a computer. Lily hadn't touched anything in the suitcase, but she did toss her sword in right before they left Los Angeles. Stacy reached for the computer and opened it, her fingers flying over the keyboard as she typed furiously. The others looked over her shoulder and waited.

"I suppose the only important thing is ..." Stacy looked at the long list of information on the screen and highlighted one piece. "There's a self-destruct code, which is the same as the password. You can activate it in two ways: with a timer or the instant-giant-explosion way."

Lily gulped. "What's the instant-giant-explosion way, exactly?" "Well, if you choose that way and close the computer, the next person who opens it gets an exploding computer." "What's the code?" Tara asked. They leaned in close to hear Stacy's barely audible whisper. "*Foveae.*"

Lily looked up. "That's a really bad code name." If Sophie got her hands on the computer, would she know the password was simply her last name?

Jake nodded. "And for a password, that sucks." Stacy's eyes darted around nervously. "Shush! We should have moved a long time ago." Stacy tucked the computer under her arm and her friends followed her down the street before the police found them. The last thing Lily wanted was to be near the wreckage of the library with police swarming the area.

Tara scaled a ladder (or it might have been another rusty fire escape) attached to the nearest building that led to the roof so she could act as a lookout while the others sat and discussed a plan.

Lily devised a way to sort their priorities. They would each say what they wanted to do, and the others would decide if it was a good idea. "Rescue the other elves," Jake said quietly. The others shook their heads. "I'm sorry, Jake, but Sophie will track us down," Lily said. Stacy kicked the wall. "Then we find Sophie. Isn't that what we've been doing this mission for?" "Yes," Lily and Jake said in unison.

"So is that our plan or isn't that plan?" Jake asked impatiently. "I mean, we've got to think fast. Sophie could be on us any second."

In that moment, Tara Aiwa slid down the ladder with a strange look on her face. "Guys, you better see this."

Chapter 67

Weapons for teddy bears

The look on Tara's face was enough to make Lily and her friends jump to their feet. "What is it?" Stacy said. "Come and see." Tara turned on her heel and scrambled up the ladder precariously, leaving the others no choice but to quickly follow. When they reached the roof, Lily whispered, "Oh, no."

The police surrounding the library were curled up on the debris-littered asphalt, cuddling their weapons and snoring audibly. The rest of New York moved around them normally, taking no notice of the strange event. "They can't see us," Jake said. "No," Stacy agreed. "If you look at an angle, you can see a faint shimmering dome surrounding the area. To the citizens, the place would look like a closed library. But anyone who was in the dome at the time the police fell asleep would see the truth."

It was then that Lily noticed someone at the scene stepping out of her car and walking around the rubble of the library, clearly confused. Jake blinked. "If that's Sophie, then what is she doing at the scene?" "But it isn't," Lily retorted. And before anyone could stop her, she was sliding down the ladder and sprinting as fast as she could towards her mother.

"Mom!" Lily grabbed her mother's shoulder and spun her around. Her mother looked at her with confused eyes. "Lily, what's wrong with the library? Why are the policemen on the ground sleeping? I was just trying to get lunch ..."

Lily decided to play out the act for all it was worth. She looked at the library for a few seconds and then looked back at her mother with a puzzled look on her face. "What do you mean? Nothing happened to the library. There's nobody sleeping on the ground. Look at it again from farther away." Lily led her mom away from the scene until they were three feet away from the edge of the dome before turning around.

The transformation of the library surprised Lily. Instead of scattered heaps of rubble and a flattened foundation with slumbering officers around it, there stood the library as it was for the past 75 years - tall with brick walls that the sunlight shone brightly on.

"Well, I guess I was dreaming," Lily's mother said with a light laugh. She crossed over to her car, said goodbye to Lily, and drove away to track down a lunch somewhere. Lily turned and saw Stacy jumping up and down and waving her arms frantically for Lily to come.

Whatever Lily's friends saw, it probably wasn't good. Lily ran as fast as she could and a minute later she was gasping for air on the roof. Once she got her air back, she coughed out, "What's wrong?"

"I just sent out a radar security check with my computer," Stacy explained. "We found something you might want to look at," Jake said. Stacy spun the computer around for Lily to see.

The screen displayed a tiny purple dot on a black background. The dot was sending out waves in every direction, but there was a yellow beacon rapidly closing in on the dot - which was basically their location. "Beacons only show up if there's someone that isn't human or an animal," Stacy said. For a while Lily and her friends stared at the screen, unable to make heads or tails of it. Suddenly, Lily felt herself yanked backward. She went sprawling on the roof. Tara knelt next to her. "Get down!" she hissed. Stacy immediately closed the computer and looked up. Jake began to rise from his sitting position, but Tara kicked at him and he fell over. "Stay low and get down the ladder," she ordered. "Sophie's coming."

That sentence brought Lily back to her senses. She crawled to the ladder and slid down, her friends following closely. They ducked into the alley from which they had come and hid behind a large dumpster as the sky darkened. The fear in the silence that came next energized the air. Lily peered out from behind the dumpster at the entrance to the alley and saw nothing. Maybe Sophie hadn't seen them. Maybe she was gone already…

A foot stepped into view and Lily held her breath, pressing her back to the dumpster. But she had the courage to look out slightly as Sophie walked past. Gray bolts of energy crackled from her fingers, causing the asphalt ground to bubble and blister. The very sight of her reminded Lily of a younger, more malicious, lady version of Emperor Palpatine. The very thought made Lily shudder. Instantly, the footsteps stopped. Lily tried to calm her jumping nerves as the footsteps started getting louder. Sophie was getting closer. Next to Lily, Stacy squeezed her eyes shut.

Sophie stopped five feet from the dumpster. Lily didn't dare look at her. She and the others held their breath and waited. Ten seconds passed. Then thirty more seconds dragged by. Lily's air was running out. Right when her lungs felt like they were going to burst, the footsteps started again, quickly going away and disappearing. Lily waited for as long as she could hold her breath before she exhaled.

Lily and her friends cautiously crept out of the alley, scanning their surroundings for any sign of danger. Tara, who had taken hold of Lily's wrist, suddenly gave a sharp cry. Lily felt her friend being yanked backward, the grip on her wrist becoming painfully tight. She whipped around just in time to see Tara fall back, disappearing into the wall, a look of surprise on her face. Soon she had disappeared completely, except for her right hand. Lily's wrist twisted as she tried to pull Tara out. But as her wrist was wrenched sideways, she was forced to release her hold...

In a matter of seconds, it all ended. Lily's hand was empty, resting against the brick wall of the building. And Tara was gone.

Chapter 68

The days to come

The next few days were quiet.

Lily's mom set off on another work trip (this time it was in Oregon), leaving Lily behind to figure out a plan. Jake and Stacy visited constantly from another hotel. Lily never opened the door until she heard one of her friends' voices. Occasionally Lily ventured outside for a little while, but danger was everywhere. Any suspicion sent Lily racing back to her apartment. Her mind was occupied during all of her waking hours, with plans, Sophie, Theresa. And Tara.

Lily had no idea where her friend was, but she hoped for the best. A week passed. Two more lagged by. Lily was starting to lose her hope. Then one day there was a knock on the door. Not loudly like Jake, or quick like Stacy. The knocks were soft, as though the person on the other side didn't want to disturb Lily. Then a voice came through, working its way to Lily's brain. "Lily? Hello?"

Lily yanked open the door and tackled Tara in a bear hug. "Tara! Where *were* you?" she exclaimed. "With Sophie," Tara explained. "*Duh.* Where's Stacy?" Tara asked. "At the hotel. Why?" It was then that a faint memory surfaced in Lily's mind. Just yesterday, Stacy had visited, complaining in distress that she'd left her computer in the alley, but when she came back to look for it, it was gone.

"Stacy lost her computer," Lily blurted. "Sophie has it," Lily's friend said. "I gave it to her a minute after I keyed in the self-destruct code. When it exploded, I escaped." "Oh." "Stacy is going to be so pissed off at me!" "But an exploding computer won't stop her from finding us," Lily said.

Thirty minutes later Tara was reunited with Jake and Stacy. Her reappearance seemed to energize Lily and the others, and soon they were crowded around Lily's desk with a map spread out on the table. "So, we have our two main assumptions," Lily said. "Sophie's either *on* this planet, or she *isn't* on this planet. Pick a guess and we'll work from there."

In the end, it was decided that Sophie probably wasn't on Earth. Lily had no idea if they were correct, but as soon as everyone guessed, Theresa called out in Lily's mind: *They are correct. I know for a fact that Sophie is on the elfin world. Lead them!*

If Theresa was going for optimism, Lily didn't like it. Nevertheless, she tried her best to secure a plan. She was doing okay until Stacy interrupted: "Lily, you're not going back on the elfin planet."

Lily glanced up. Stacy was telling the truth and she knew it. They all knew it. But was it right for her to send her friends back to their home planet into a war that was beyond their knowledge to defeat? "If you're sure, then you can go back. But you will visit, right?" Dead silence filled the air as another thought dawned on Lily. "You're not coming back," she realized. "Theresa's moving the planet far away, out of Sophie's reach. That way, no harm will come to us or our people. And you will probably be safe, too," Tara said quietly. "I know we're leaving a bit early." Jake fidgeted with the edge of his shirt sleeve as he spoke. "But we've all realized a long time ago that spring will be too late for us to leave." "It'll be okay," Stacy said. "We'll try our best to communicate with you."

That thought was barely enough to lift Lily's spirits. "Can you Skype me?" she asked hopefully. Tara nodded. "That wouldn't be beyond Theresa's powers, would it?"

"No, it wouldn't." Lily considered the pros and cons of her friends leaving. Sophie would certainly send in more attacks, for sure, but at least Stacy and the others would be safe.

Safe. Lily hadn't experienced that feeling for the past few months. But if her friends would be safe, she wasn't going to stop them.

"Okay, then." Lily stood up. "Get packed."

Chapter 69

Goodbyes, hellos and important calls

The next morning Theresa made one final appearance. Lily bid her friends farewell and stood next to her bed as Theresa surrounded her friends in wispy magic. Right before they were completely obscured, the sorceress turned to Lily. Her face wore the gentle, if less mischievous, smile she gave Lily when they first met. "Lilith Claire, you are the most special person I've ever met. I think we can afford to Skype you soon. And remember - I'm watching you." And with a playful wink, the magic completely covered them, and they were gone.

Lily took hold of her suitcase - the elves' last gift to her. She would have to use the equipment inside sparingly. She immediately set off to work, devising the best plan she could think of. In the end, it wasn't surprising when Lily's mother came back from her work trip five hours later to find her daughter sound asleep on her bed, one arm draped over a brown suitcase.

When Lily woke up, sunlight was streaming through the open window. Lily stretched luxuriously and grabbed her suitcase. There was a loud trembling sound, coming from the direction of the harbor. Careful not to wake her mother, Lily crept out of her room and down the stairs, but as soon as she was outside, she made a beeline to the harbor, a glittering blue-gray expanse a quarter mile away. For a second, she looked around unsteadily. Had she forgotten her plan already? Then she remembered what she had to do and pulled her phone out of her pocket to make an important call. Years ago, her 23-year old friend had enrolled in the military in the Special Operations Department - which meant she wasn't sent to battles, but to strange disturbances in surrounding cities. Two rings later, someone picked up the phone on the other side. "Hello?" "Anna, it's me." "Don't call me Anna!"

Lily sighed. "Hello, *Ann*. There isn't much difference in that name, anyway!" "That's better. What have you been up to lately, Lily?" "What have *you* been up to?" "Well, I'm in a team heading towards New York Harbor right now. Apparently, there's been a strange disturbance coming from there."

Lily's heart did a hundred jumping jacks. "You can't go there." Anna's voice sounded slightly exasperated. "Why not?" "Because I'm the only one who knows what's in the harbor." "Lily, I don't have time for your jokes-"

On the other side of the line, Lily gripped her phone tighter. "Anna, I've been in exactly two more battles than you between two different worlds. I wish I had time to explain, but I'm at the harbor right now with a bunch of dangerous stuff waiting for what's in the water to come out. Don't stop me." Lily hung up quickly before Anna could contradict her.

Now was the time for her to put her plan into action, before Anna's team or whatever was in the harbor could stop her. As Lily reached for the zipper of her suitcase, the ground rumbled. Lily froze and looked up in shock as something rose out of the harbor.

Chapter 69: Goodbyes, hellos and important calls

It took Lily five seconds to take in the scene. By then half of the harbor had begun to churn. Fear shot through her and she ran, clutching her suitcase, sprinting away from the snarling creatures that crawled out of the water. These were no regular animals. Lily had a feeling that Sophie created them and then set them loose to destroy the city. They were reptilian, about six feet tall on their hind legs, long black claws scraping the sand and pulling them out of the harbor. As the first five monsters dragged themselves onto the beach lining the harbor, the army arrived.

Anna was the first person to step out of the military-style van closest to Lily. At the sight of the creatures, her mouth dropped open in shock. But then she raised her gun. "Don't shoot!" Lily cried. She had to get out of the way before they started firing.

Anna stared at Lily, her gun lowering. Lily wondered if her friend still recognized her, after two years apart. "Ann, please. Do *not* fire," Lily ordered slowly. But then Anna's expression hardened and raising her weapon, she fired a whole round in her direction.

It all happened so quickly. The bullets flew over her shoulder, slamming into the chest of the beast that was about to sink its claws into Lily. The horrible creature fell backward, gurgling, thrashing violently until its eyes glassed over and it went limp. But already another wave of monsters was crawling out of the water.

Anna holstered her gun and drew her laser ray shooter. Lily opened her suitcase and wrenched out her sword. She then dropped the suitcase at Anna's feet, told her to be *very* careful with its contents, and sprinted into the front line of the beasts.

The first ten minutes of battle was filled with howls of pain and the smell of burnt flesh as the Special Operations team fired their deadly lasers into the creatures. Lily fought with her sword, deflecting stray lasers before they hit her and directing them into the monsters' flesh. But wave after wave of lizards (there really was no other way to describe them) crawled out of the water to face the small team of people. But there was just too much of them. First one, then two lizards got past the lasers and stumbled over the cars, the vehicles buckling under their weight. Lily knew they would keep coming from the water, from the source that brought them to life.

She managed to get to the waterline without a single claw scratch. She held her breath and dove underwater, swimming with smooth, precise strokes, as her father had taught her when she was young. The clear water made an easy view of the lizards coming wave after wave out of the water. Her mother said that the harbor was once heavily polluted, but special filters had cleansed the water. Lily swam upwards, grabbed a big breath of air and dove again. Her sword reflected the sunlight, acting like a flashlight. But as she swam deeper, the water seemed to become lighter, like she was going towards a big light.

Curious, Lily propelled herself through the water a little further. Two seconds later, she dropped abruptly, crashing into the ground. "Oof!"

It was her voice that surprised her the most. Not muffled like it should be underwater, but loud and clear. A second later, Lily realized that she could breathe, despite being at the bottom of the harbor. After a careful examination of her surroundings, she found out that there was a bubble of oxygen surrounding her. She stood on a hill of perfectly dry sand. And in the center of the dome was a tall building from which the lizards emerged. Lily adjusted her grip on her sword and decided it was a good idea to check it out.

Chapter 70

A very important bubble pops

As soon as Lily placed her foot on the marble floor, a lizard zipped out through the doors. She barely managed to flatten herself against the wall to avoid being run over. Keeping her back against the wall, Lily successfully got inside without another 900-pound lizard smashing into her. In the dim light, she could tell she was in a big room, with nothing but a small glass replica of the bubble that surrounded the building in the middle of the floor. The lizards came from a hole directly in front of it, crawling out so fast if you blinked they were already gone. They came out one by one in a crowded line. Lily skirted behind the monsters to where the bubble lay. She realized that there was a very tiny model of a building inside in the center of the bubble - which meant the bubble was probably connected to something important.

She considered the consequences. The bubble sculpture obviously represented the oxygen dome around the building. If it popped, about fifty tons of water would come crashing down on her. But fifty tons of water was heavy enough to crush a lizard flat, especially if the building collapsed. Lily braced herself and kicked the bubble into the wall.

The bubble broke silently. Lily could hear the deafening sounds of water crashing down from outside. She knew she had only five seconds to leave, ten at the most. Lily made a mad dash for the double doors as the back of the building caved in. Her shoes slipped on the polished marble as she kept her eyes on her path. She no longer cared about the 900-pound lizards. All she wanted to do was save herself.

Lily sprinted through the doors and hit the cold water like a brick in her face as the rest of the tower collapsed into a cloud of debris and swirling dust. Where the building entrance was, there was nothing but a large slab of stone. Lily had a feeling the hole was gone, wiped out of existence. Well, there was nothing else to do underwater. Besides, her air was running out. Lily swam for the surface.

Lily's fears were confirmed as she dragged herself onto the shore. The day had turned scalding-hot, and New York City was overrun by the monstrous lizards. What used to be the Special Operations team was scattered near the edge of the harbor, lying on the ground. It didn't take long for Lily to find Anna, who stumbled over to her. "What on earth was *that*?" Anna demanded. "I suppose they were 900-pound lizards," Lily answered. Anna sighed and walked away to help carry injured soldiers to the ambulances.

Lily knew at once that she alone couldn't stop them. The monsters, tearing into buildings with their razor-sharp long claws, joining the chorus of screams from the people with their own battle cries: a scratchy screeching sound that sent everyone running for their lives and hiding. The army had arrived, hundreds of uniformed men and women shooting into the monsters' ranks. But by the time you brought down the lizard in front of you, another one had leaped over the corpse and sank its claws into you. Lily tried her best, using a laser gun from a fallen soldier she found nearby, sitting on rooftops and directing the deadly rays into her targets.

Shortly after, Lily saw a man in a suit walking into an old abandoned apartment, flanked by bodyguards - a man she recognized. She immediately started forming a plan in her mind, leaping across the building rooftops towards the apartment. If anybody had enough patience to listen to her, the President did.

Lily followed the President and his guards down a hallway into a small room. As the man sat down for a conference meeting, Lily stepped into view. "President Johnson!" Guns were turned towards her instantly, but the President yelled, "Stop!"

George Johnson eyed her. "What do you want?" Lily stepped forward carefully. "Your armies aren't enough to stop the invasion." One of the number one rules when meeting the President in person: *don't* insult him if there are six bodyguards behind you. Lily heard weapons cock, but the President's face only took on a look of concentration. "Go on." The words tumbled out of Lily's mouth before she could stop them. "The lizards - they're at least 900 pounds each. They easily outnumber your forces."

"The army can stop these creatures. They have already sent out thousands of soldiers, and one of them is the 1st lieutenant's daughter herself," Peterson said. Lily's anger grew. "Ok. Fine. Well, how about you tell your 1st lieutenant this: his daughter Anna and her team were attacked viciously and defeated by the lizards. You can go and ask her; she'll tell you the truth." The President threw up his hands. "Fine. We'll discuss this issue."

Lily knew the President had seen her before - her father was a world-famous businessman running around 24/7 to answer his boss's (aka President George Johnson) calls. He sighed heavily. "What's your name?" Lily expected the question: a quick security check. "Lily Claire," she answered. A computer-wielding lady sitting next to President Peterson looked up. "You're lying. There's no current citizen of New York City with that name."

Lily tried again. "Lilith Claire. Lily's my nickname." The lady nodded. "Ah." "So ..." the President said, "how do we stop these creatures?" Lily looked around and surveyed the people in the room. "Mr. President, if you don't mind, I'd like to speak with you alone."

Chapter 71

The truth

Lily told him everything: the whole account of her daring adventures, from when she disappeared from school to now. For the whole time she'd been with the elves, Lily always imagined she would be telling her mother first and now here she was, saying her story to the President himself instead, George Johnson.

After she had finished speaking, President Johnson said, "You still haven't told me how to defeat the lizards." Lily sighed. "I *don't* know how to defeat the lizards. *That's* the problem. And nobody can actually get close enough to one of those beasts without seriously jeopardizing their lives." For a while, she and the President stared gloomily at a computer on the table, which displayed the rapidly rising number of fallen soldiers.

A soft *plunk* caught their attention. They looked up to find a small sphere the size of an orange sitting in the center of the table, gently flashing light gray. Lily's sword was instantly in her hand. "Don't touch it," she said. But she found her sword sliding back into its sheath as she spotted the note in front of the sphere - a small piece of paper that read: *One last gift to defeat them all. I'm still counting on you, Lily. –Theresa.*

"What does that mean? *One last gift to defeat them all?*" the President asked. Lily looked up. She knew what the gift was. "It's a shock grenade. When detonated, it'll send out a wave to rinse the entire city - a last attempt to override Sophie's powers. Every living thing within a five-mile radius ... dies."

As the President silently nodded in understanding, Lily thought of how Theresa had worded her sentence: a gift that would defeat them all. *Defeat them all.* Did she mean just the lizards that were raiding the city? No. Then she remembered that if Sophie or Theresa created something and it was destroyed, their life force weakened. And she realized that this was no ordinary grenade from Theresa. Making so many lizards would have taken almost all of Sophie's energy. If she pressed the detonation button, not just the lizards would die. Sophie would, too.

Lily took the bomb and gingerly put it in her pocket. "We're out of time. The lizards might be coming for us as I speak." As if on cue, a loud BOOM shook the building. President Peterson grabbed his computer and shut it, following Lily out of the room.

Lily gave the President one last message before they parted: "Evacuate the whole city and get them out as fast as you can. I'll give you an hour. When you're done, signal me. Get a pair of binoculars if you need to find me." Then she ran down the hall away from the President, out of the building to join the battle.

Lily spent most of her time running from the lizards. The remaining soldiers, upon being given new orders, had left with the citizens. As the minutes passed by, Lily climbed a building to do a quick check of the city to make sure that absolutely no one was left. To her right, Lily saw a flash flare shoot up, alerting her that she was the only citizen left in New York City. She turned and saw the giant crowd that was the population of New York City standing fifty yards away from the five-mile line. And suddenly Lily realized that they were waiting for her - waiting for her to succeed and bring safety back to the area.

She could only hope that her plan would work. She reminded herself that she was doing this job, this incredibly important job, for her friends, and her family, and her people. Lily was too far away to get out in time, but if she ran and threw the grenade as far as she could, she might just make it.

Lily spent the last ten minutes or so going back to the harbor and grabbing her suitcase from where it lay in the sand. The equipment inside was untouched, but the value of the items was priceless.

Her hour was up. Lily kept running, searching for a good place to throw the grenade. She finally found a spot, at the top of a high hill, where she could throw it down and far away from the location. Theresa had told her that she was still counting on her.

Lily wasn't going to let her friend down.

She took a deep breath, pressed the detonation button, and lobbed it as far as she could.

Chapter 72

The escape

As the grenade left her grasp, Lily realized that there was a flaw in her plan.

She realized that she had miscalculated her distance from the line of safety. There was no way she could cross that line in time. The grenade sailed farther and farther down.

Two voices exploded in her mind: *NO!* Two crackling waves of gray sped towards the grenade. Sophie wanted to save her own life, and Theresa wanted to save Lily's. Theresa had seen the flaw of the plan too and knew that Lily's life was at risk. But Lily knew it was too late, that she would never reach safety in time, as the grenade burst against the ground far below, sending out a massive gray wave that hurtled towards her at an amazing speed.

Lily could see the lizards falling limp in the streets as the wave sped towards her. Sophie's magic disappeared into thin air. Theresa's misty bolt of gray flipped direction and zoomed back towards Lily, but the wave was already ahead of her. Lily saw that there was no use to run away. She faced her doom and waited. Every single muscle in her body screamed, *Run*! But she kept her feelings in check and stared at the wave of death and Theresa's magic, wondering which one would reach her first.

Theresa's misty wave caught up just as the bomb's shockwave hit Lily. She fell and her eyes closed, her sword and suitcase falling from her hands and settling in the grass at the top of the hill.

***

Lily was dreaming.

She knew it from the instant six misty figures appeared in the black background of her sleep. Her friends stepped towards her.

"Am I ..." Lily couldn't even form the words to her question. Tara shook her head. "No, Lily. Theresa's magic reached you just in time. You have fallen into a deep sleep. Theresa thinks you should wake up soon."

The wispy gray form that was Oneida fiddled with the edge of her shirt. "You did great, Lily. Everyone knows that. The damage to your home city would have been much worse if it wasn't for you."

A sudden thought struck Lily. "But Sophie ..." she said. Theresa shook her head. "Sophie is gone," she said quietly. "Our planet and your planet are both safe, thanks to you," Jake said. "To our people, you will be forever remembered as a hero," Stacy smiled gently. "And just so you know, Skype us whenever you want to, but Jake might accidentally drop and break the computer before that happens." Parker elbowed Jake playfully.

Theresa said, "Lily, it'll all be fine. The people have started to move back in. You're in the hospital. Your family's waiting for you to wake up. It's time you return to the real world. Perhaps you should tell them the truth, just as you did to the President." Her friends gathered together. "Goodbye, Lily," they all said in unison. They smiled and disappeared, and Lily opened her eyes.

She was in a hospital, all right. About ten different doctors were staring down at her. Her mom, brother, and dad were standing next to her.

Lily's precious suitcase lay on a table next to her bed, and her sword was carefully placed on top. Everyone was looking at her with a mixture of concern and relief on her faces.

Lily processed this all in less than ten seconds. She wanted to leap out of her bed and embrace her family, but her entire being was weak.

She looked up. She had spent so much time away from them that she didn't know what to say. *Hello. Sorry for the giant invasion that hit New York, but I got it taken care of. No worries!*

Then Lily realized that she didn't need a long message to say. Something simple would be good enough.

"Hey, guys." Lily smiled.

Epilogue

"Guys, come on." Lily grabbed her friend Adaline and walked out of the building. Finally, twenty years after the war, she had joined the Special Operations Department, where her mentor Anna worked. Her elfin friends still sent messages to her from the strange world where they came from, and she always replied back. But no mission of any size could compare to the brutal wars that Lily experienced when she was a teenager.

They stood on a hill overlooking the whole of New York City. Lily had asked the army herself to build the army building on the very hill where she had faced her doom years ago. And now Lily, with her friend and the other people that were in her team, scanned the city below, as they always did on a mission.

"There," Adaline said, pointing. Not too far from where they stood, a giant serpent with the frilled head of a dragon rose out of the harbor thrashing in the cold water. Ever since Sophie died, the pool of magic from which the lizards emerged long ago stirred in the harbor, making new monsters with no orders but to destroy. The missions were hard but in the end all the beasts were lying motionless on the ground.

In other words, it was just like old times.

"Ready?" Lily asked. Her team nodded. "All right, then." She raised her voice to a shout. "You want to destroy, huh? Come and get us!" Raising their weapons, they yelled like banshees and charged.

About the Author

Laura T. Lee is a 10-year-old author. She was born in Massachusetts, United States. She is inspired to write from reading books written by many popular authors, including Rick Riordan, J.K. Rowling and Suzanne Collins. She writes action-packed funny fantasy stories. Her 12-year-old brother, David T. Lee, is an author of four published books. All of their books are available for purchase online, including Amazon.com and Barnesandnoble.com.

If you would like to learn more about Laura and David's writing journey, please use the link below:

http://booksrfun.infomages.com/

Social media

 www.facebook.com/infomages.BooksRFun

 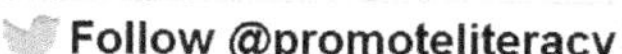

 www.pinterest.com/infomages

www.youtube.com/infomages

 promoteliteracy.tumblr.com/